Murder makes the Ballot

CHARMAIN Z. BRACKETT

DIAMOND KEY PRESS

Published July 2018

Dedicated to the beautiful city of Augusta with its rich history and legends with a special mention to the notorious Haunted Pillar, which met its demise in December 2016. In a twist of fate, the driver, who struck the pillar and toppled it to the ground, credited the cursed pillar with saving his life.

Special thanks to all of the amazing Augusta artists who allowed me to use them in this novel. All of the artists mentioned are real people; the rest of the characters are simply that, fictional and any resemblance to anyone living or dead is purely coincidental.

Reach Charmain Z. Brackett at www.facebook.com/thekeyofelyon or @CZBrackett on Twitter.

1

I sat in my car and waited.

I had arrived too early. Part of me was hopeful, but the other part of me dreaded this meeting. I knew I shouldn't be anxious about seeing someone who had been a good friend, probably my best friend, but I was. Since the birth of Dana's baby, Lily, six months ago - and even before that - I'd pulled away from my friend when she needed me most as I tried to figure out my own life. I knew I'd been selfish, and although I regretted it, I didn't know how to make things right between us.

She had called me about a week ago. Her cheating husband, Bill, was now running for mayor. Yes, mayor! I couldn't believe it. She asked me to help decorate a fancy soiree they were holding at the Old Government House, and I said "yes" mainly out of a guilty conscience. But I regretted that answer from the time I hung up the phone.

So, there I sat - half watching the traffic on Telfair Street and the other half gazing at the beautiful, historic building. All the while, I wondered what I'd gotten myself into. I picked up my phone to pass the time and found a website describing the structure. I filled my brain with trivia, trying to delay the inevitable - and most likely, uncomfortable - reunion with Dana. I was hopeful her husband wasn't going to be there, but I had a feeling he would be. Maybe it was Bill that I dreaded seeing and not Dana.

I sighed and glanced at my phone.

Built around 1801, the Old Government House was designed in the Federal style of architecture with balconies, a wrought-iron portico and floor-to-ceiling windows. It was a beautiful place that served as Augusta's first courthouse but later was the home to one of the city's first mayors, a newspaper editor, and a prominent mill owner. It wound up back in the city's hands in the late 1980s and is used for small receptions and weddings.

The outside of the building was beautifully landscaped with a massive magnolia in the front in addition to the second-largest gingko tree in the United States. The gingko was planted in honor of George Washington's visit to the Garden City in 1791. Yes, George Washington did actually sleep in our fair city. There were several historic markers to attest to that.

Multiple azaleas and camellias also adorned the landscape, but in October, none of them were in bloom.

The sound of a blaring train horn only two blocks away and the rumbling of the train as it lumbered through downtown Augusta jolted me back to reality. I checked the time once again. I'd wasted 10 minutes researching the building's history. I still had 10 minutes to burn. I moved my car to the parking lot behind the building and slowly made my way to my meeting with Dana.

As soon as I entered, I overheard Dana and Bill in a heated argument.

"I promised I'd back you in this, but not if you're cheating on me again."

"Dana, sweetheart, I swear to you on my grandmother's grave that I am not cheating on you. It's all a big misunderstanding. I love you, Dana, and I really need you in my corner."

"You've already humiliated me more than once, Bill. I've heard all the other rumors about you. I was stupid to take you back all those times. What was I thinking?"

"Dana, I love you and our baby. Please don't say things like that."

I could hear the desperation in his voice. I wasn't sure if he meant it, but I could tell he didn't want her to leave, whether he loved her or not.

"People warned me about you. I should've listened. I'm going to call Grace and tell her not to come."

I don't think I could ever remember Dana sounding that angry, and I'd known her practically from the cradle.

"Ah, your friend, Grace, who never even bothered to check on you."

His tone was sharp.

"Bill, do you really want her husband to come to her rescue once again?"

"I can handle Drew."

Her laugh mocked him.

"You handle Drew? That's a joke. From what I remember, he didn't like the way you treated his wife and put you in your place and good."

"Just because he's a cop doesn't mean I'm afraid of him."

Dana's laugh mocked Bill.

There was a pause.

"I know why she did what she did," Dana continued. Her tone had changed. Her voice was softer, but it still carried. "She was supposed to have a baby around the same time Lily was born. She didn't tell anyone; she was waiting until the right time; the time when she was pretty sure she wouldn't lose her baby. But Grace lost her baby again, and the doctors don't give her much hope of ever having a child of her own, according to what her mother has told my mother. I totally understand because I was in her position once. Yes, it hurt me that she wasn't there when Lily was born, but I get it. I was that way once, wanting to be happy for your friends, but at the same time, your own pain getting in the way. You don't seem to remember that. You're a man. You'll never understand, so you need to stop judging her."

I wiped away the tears. I'd never told her any of that, but it made things a little easier for me. I didn't hate myself as much.

Scratch that, I still hated myself. I felt awkward listening in on this conversation. I wasn't sure what to do but eavesdrop.

"Do you forgive me, Dana?"

"You're hanging by a thread as it is, Bill, and I swear to you, if I find out you're lying to me again and cheating, I'll kill you myself."

My jaw dropped. I'd never heard Dana threaten anyone, and in that tone, she sounded like she would do it.

"I'm not talking about it anymore," Dana's tone was icy. "Grace will be here any minute, and I don't want her to know we're fighting."

I stepped back outside and counted to 15 before walking in. Dana was waiting on me. Her face had transformed into the Dana I'd always known, not the angry beast I'd overheard.

"Grace, I'm so glad you came," she said as she hugged me.

She looked perfect.

"I have a few ideas for how I want this is event to go, and I need your best designs," she said as she guided me around the historic building.

Bill grimaced.

"Good morning, Mrs. Ward," he said in a snarky tone that meant Dana had ordered him to be nice to me.

Bill didn't say anything else; he barely glanced at me and acted as though they hadn't fought, but he didn't share her poker face. He scowled and looked away every time I glanced his way. All I could remember was the time during the annual Masters Tournament that he came into my shop asking for flowers, and he let me have it. He might have been thinking the same thing for all I knew. I did know Drew had confronted him about it. After a few uncomfortable moments, Bill left the room.

"This won't be a huge gathering. It may be 50 or 75 people at the most. The men won't care about the flowers, but we don't always have to impress them. The ladies can write checks, too, and sometimes, they have a little more clout, if you know what I mean."

I smiled at her.

"And it's really not a political function, just a small party. No money changing hands at this event. That's later. We just want them to start thinking about contributions to his campaign. He's just trying to raise support."

She wanted a couple of large, over-the-top designs, something people would talk about after the event.

"I know you're the right one for this, Grace," she stopped and stared at me. "You've never let me down."

With that, tears began to burn in my eyes because I knew I had let her down. I wasn't there when she needed me most. I tried to look away, but she reached out to hug me.

"I did let you down. I wasn't there for you when Lily was born, and I'll never forgive myself for that."

"Grace, I understand more than you know. You were there so many times for me, and I was so happy that I didn't even see one of my best friends was going through the hardest time in her life."

"Stop, or I'm going to have to start calling you 'Saint Dana.' You were supposed to be happy. You deserved to be happy. We were just supposed to be happy together," I tried to laugh as I wiped the tears away.

"I'm not a saint. We both know that," she smiled. "But I did the exact same thing at one time. I should've recognized it. Why are we talking about that? That's water under the bridge now. I've been without you for too long."

She linked her arm with mine. I couldn't believe she was being so understanding. Though it was like her, it felt odd for some reason.

"I never told you that I was there when Drew put Bill in his place. It was eye-opening. Drew loves you more than you could ever imagine, Grace. You're a blessed woman. I wish I could say the same."

"Thank you."

I wasn't sure how to respond to her final comment, but my mother always told me just to say "thank you" to compliments and leave them at that. The confrontation between Drew and Bill was in

April after Drew had solved his first case as a homicide detective. My husband was a different man then. He'd started going to counseling. He'd stopped drinking. He was the man I'd married. He was different now.

"Call me with the price, and plan on being here around 5:30 next Friday."

"Sounds great."

"And then you and I are going to get together, okay?"

"Yes."

"Promise?"

"I promise, Dana."

She gave me another hug before I left. I took a deep breath as I walked out of the Old Government House. I knew just the person who needed to create the arrangement, and it wasn't me. It was Emmie. She was another person I'd barely seen or spoken to in the past few months. Ever since she started her temporary job as a sketch artist with the FBI, she was so busy, and I missed her.

Back at the shop, it was quiet. It was always quiet now. I guess rumors had gotten out that if Grace was at your event, there could be a dead body nearby. I wasn't sure where business had gone. Jazzy was in school and only worked a few hours a week. Beth had been traveling out of the country a lot. I hadn't seen Jimmy Hughes in a couple of months, and business was slow. Truth be told, I needed Dana and her small party. I needed more business overall.

I stared at my cell phone, debating on calling Emmie. I didn't know if I could afford to pay her. Instead, I sent her a text that simply said hello, I miss you, friend.

About 30 minutes later, I heard the bells chime as someone opened the door. I walked out of my office to see Emmie standing there with a plastic bag. It was strange for her to come through the front door. She usually came in the back.

"I think someone needs ice cream therapy," she said with a smile. She put the bag on the counter.

"How did you -"

Emmie put her hands on her hips and cocked her head to the side.

"How many times have I told you that you aren't the only one who knows things, sweetie?" she asked with a raised eyebrow.

"You got all that from five words?"

She nodded.

"I've been feeling it, too, and I should've called a couple of weeks ago. I just been so busy," she said.

She paused before shaking her head.

"I need a friend. This FBI gig is harder than I thought it was going to be," she said, trying to manage a smile. "So, do I need to break out the spoons here or do you want to meet me at my house? The boys are with their dad tonight."

I looked at the clock. Her timing was perfect, of course. It was almost closing time.

"Drew will probably be home late tonight, so let me lock up, and I'll be right over."

It didn't take long to get to Emmie's from the shop. She was in the kitchen scooping up the ice cream when I came in. There was no need to knock. We'd been friends for so long.

"It's been a chocolate chip cookie dough kind of couple of months," said Emmie as she thrust the bowl of ice cream into my hands. "Eat up, I bought two containers, and I even have extra chocolate syrup if you'd like."

"It's been that bad, huh?"

"I thought I could do this," she said as she walked from the kitchen into the living room, where she plopped down on her couch and pulled her legs underneath her. I followed her lead. It felt good to take my shoes off.

"I thought I'd be doing something with my art, but in my delusional state, I forgot that I would be dealing with crime scenes and dead bodies. I remembered the reason I didn't pursue the medical field."

"I'm sorry, Emmie."

"The children are the hardest. Reconstructing faces for those tiny skeletons," she paused and shook her head. "I had no idea people could do the things they do to children. Some of those things make me sick to even think about. I just don't know how people can be so evil."

"I have no idea."

Emmie paused and got that look – the one where she wanted to ask me something, but she wasn't sure what to say. We'd been friends forever, so I knew it well.

"So, I wanted to ask you if I could do that art exhibit that you've been pushing me to do. "

"Of course! That invitation is always open. Just tell me when, and we'll make it happen."

"I've had to use my art as therapy lately and get out all of the yuck that I've seen. I saw this documentary and the guy who used his art as therapy said, 'I was a sponge full of icky' and his art wrung out the icky on the inside. I feel that way. The art draws out the yuck and makes me feel clean again."

"You have things ready?"

"Lots of things. I'll show you after I finish this," she said, shoveling a heaping spoonful of ice cream in her mouth. "I don't want it to melt."

I laughed at her. Emmie always knew how to make me do that. She smiled, but she was staring dead at me. She knew something was up, so her smile faded with her next statement.

"Tell me what's going on with you, sweetie."

And with that, I couldn't smile anymore.

"Business hasn't been the greatest. Maybe an art show would bring some exposure to the shop, and I need your help for a party next Friday if there's any way you can, Emmie."

"What kind of party?"

"Bill Andrews is planning a run for mayor."

She started coughing and sputtering. I wasn't sure how you could choke on ice cream, but Emmie found a way. Then she started laughing.

"Bill as in that two-timing slime bag? You've got to be kidding me."

"Yes, the same; and no, I'm not kidding."

"You'd seriously consider helping him?"

"Not him. Dana."

"You've finally been in touch with Dana?"

I nodded.

"I saw her today."

"Bill's running for mayor," she shook her head with every word. I think she was trying to let it all sink in. I knew she couldn't believe it, and as much of a swine as he was, he had a great chance of becoming mayor. He had a charming personality - to those who didn't know him well.

Augusta had had more than its fair share of corrupt politicians over the years. Having someone like Bill in office wouldn't be unusual. Well, I don't think anyone actually had been as horrible as Bill. At least, I hoped not. He topped that list as far as I was concerned, though corruption in Richmond County went back as far as anyone could remember and then some. Augusta author Berry Fleming even wrote about it in the 1940s in a novel called Col. Effingham's Raid. Though it was set in a fictional Georgia town, everyone knew it was all about political corruption in Augusta. It was even made into a film starring Charles Coburn and Joan Bennett. Despite Fleming's protests, the shenanigans of the good ole boy corrupt political machine continued for years with more than one local politician winding up in jail. Bill had the charm and had managed to weasel out of every sticky situation he'd ever come across. Why did I think this would be any different?

Crony politics was alive and well. Oh, Augusta had its share of racial divides, but Bill somehow managed to cross those lines as well. I don't know how he did it. Maybe he was paying people.

After several moments of shaking her head, she looked at me.

"I'll help you, sweetie, but there are only two reasons I'll do it.

One is I need to touch flowers again, and the second is that it's you."

I gave her a hug.

"Thanks for being my friend. Now, let me see your paintings."

Emmie had several pieces she'd worked on. Some were abstract; others were of landscapes and beaches.

"These are beautiful. We need to do this."

2

I didn't stay at Emmie's long. I was home by 7:30, but Drew was not. We had eaten our ice cream and had a chance to reconnect, but I couldn't tell her everything going on with me. Some things I still buried deep inside. She didn't ask, and I didn't tell.

I took a hot bath and crawled into bed before 9. Sleep was an escape for me. I hadn't had any dreams in several months - a welcome relief. I actually looked forward to resting at night.

But tonight would be different. Tonight, they would start again. If I'd known, I wouldn't have been looking forward to sleep.

The dream was hazy at first, but then Bill Andrews came into view. He was wearing a white dinner jacket, black bow tie, black pants. He was smiling, schmoozing, being charming, but in an instant, that changed. His face twisted in pain as blood began to pour out of his chest onto his white shirt. He put his hand over his heart and pulled his hand back. It was drenched in crimson. Then, he fell to his knees and landed facedown. I looked up. I saw Dana standing there; she shrieked and knelt in the puddle of her husband's blood. She was wearing a gold dress that quickly soaked up the pool as she shook him and screamed his name.

I woke up in a cold sweat and bolted into a seated position.

I closed my eyes. I had to take in everything about that dream before I forgot the small details. I needed to write it down. I couldn't see where we were in it, but I assumed it was at the party she'd asked me to create the arrangements for.

I looked at the clock. It was a little after 2 a.m. I couldn't exactly call Dana at this hour.

Drew was in bed beside me, but he didn't stir. I think he was out cold. I got up and walked into the living room to write the dream down. If this was a warning, could I stop it? Would anyone listen to me? The second thought was the most common one I had.

"God, is this a blessing or a curse? For once would someone listen to me?"

It seemed like I'd had these dreams all my life. Sometimes they were glimpses into the future; sometimes, they gave me ideas on how to work my business; sometimes, they were just insights into people's character. My church friends, the ones who didn't think I was crazy, thought they were a gift from God, and everyone else, well, they just thought I was crazy. So, I didn't share them with many people.

I whispered the words of a prayer. I had to tell Dana. She would understand. Though I didn't like Bill, I didn't want him dead. He could have his pride wounded or he could change, but I didn't want him dead. It would be too horrible to see another murder scene. Why did people have to die when I was delivering flowers? Funerals were one thing. Florists were supposed to be part of funerals, but I'd had enough of crime scenes. I had been seeing a therapist for a few months. It really helped, but the bills became too much so I stopped going. Drew had started taking money out of the account. I knew where it was going. Fortunately, he wasn't on my business account, so he couldn't touch that money. I couldn't tell my therapist everything. I didn't tell her much about my dreams, and I didn't tell her too much about Drew's problems. I was afraid to. Even with doctor-patient confidentiality, I couldn't tell her everything.

I fell asleep on the couch trying to figure out what to do. I wondered about Dana. She was so quick on the scene, and I'd heard the things she'd said to Bill. I couldn't see Dana as a murderer. I wondered how he died. I didn't hear a gunshot. I didn't see a murder weapon, but there was no doubt he was dead. There was too much blood.

I woke up the next morning on the couch with Drew staring at me from the nearby chair.

"Good morning, stranger."

"Guilty, Grace. I'm guilty as charged. What are you doing out here?"

"Hard night," I sat up. I needed some food. I think I had a sugar hangover. I was reluctant to tell Drew about the dream. He never stopped me from talking about my dreams, but he still wasn't overly anxious to hear about them. I wasn't sure what kind of response I'd get from him. He hadn't been himself for a few weeks, well, months. Lately it was harder. I knew why. I found myself walking on eggshells again.

"Are you hungry? I think I could go for some eggs," I said as I got up and started to walk to the kitchen. Drew touched my arm.

"What happened to you last night?"

"What do you mean?"

"You're answering questions with questions again," he said.

I smiled.

"I'm fine."

He stepped closer to me, his eyes scanning my face as though he was trying to figure me out. I broke away from his gaze as he repeated his question.

"What happened to you last night?"

When I returned to look at him, he raised an eyebrow at me. I smiled.

"I went to Emmie's, and we had ice cream. I think I ate too much."

He nodded.

"You sent me a text last night, so I knew that much. I mean what brought you out here? When I got home, you were in bed."

"Just couldn't sleep is all."

"What did you dream?"

I hesitated. It was gruesome, and I wondered if it was one

of those dreams - the ones that came true. Maybe it wasn't. And this morning he seemed genuinely interested. I wasn't sure what to make of it.

"Who said anything about a dream?"

He raised an eyebrow.

"How long have we been married?"

"It was nothing."

"I don't believe that, either."

I took a deep breath as I replayed the images in my head.

"I saw Bill Andrews die."

I gave him all the details of the dream, and he took several deep breaths.

"I can't stand the guy," I said. I wanted to laugh the dream off. "Maybe it was just a subconscious reaction, and I murdered him in my dream to save Augusta from him becoming mayor."

I tried to make light of it, but Drew shook his head and furrowed his brow.

"Grace, how many people have you killed in your dreams?"

"None."

"How many have you seen dead?"

"Just the bodies I've found and …" I trailed off and lowered my voice. "And Mark and Linda."

He took a deep breath and let it out slowly. His temples bulged as he gritted his teeth. I'd hit a nerve whenever I mentioned their names. I wanted him to talk about that night, but obviously this wasn't the time or place. The anniversary of their deaths was approaching, and I was worried about what was going on inside Drew. I knew there was turmoil. He had never faced their deaths. He'd never dealt with his emotions. He ignored things, letting them fester. Well, he didn't ignore them; he tried to drown them. I knew he'd started drinking heavily again. He tried to hide it, but the only person he was deceiving was himself. He tried to keep working business as usual, but I knew there was more under the surface. I looked away. I was afraid of setting him off. I never knew what would do that.

"I'm hungry, Drew. Would you like some breakfast?"

I walked into the kitchen. As I pulled a frying pan out from the cabinet, he touched my arm again. He had a stunned look on his face.

"Wait a minute. Did you say Bill wants to become mayor?"

I laughed.

"It took you that long to put those words together."

I pulled out some eggs, cheese, and tomatoes for the omelets I was going to make. He grabbed a knife and took the tomatoes from me.

"Bill and mayor. I hope Augusta's voters are smarter than that."

"I guess I haven't seen you to tell you that Bill is planning a run for mayor, and Dana asked me to do the flowers for a party they are having in a couple of days."

"Maybe he was killed at this event?"

"I'm not sure. I couldn't tell where it was, but this will be a swanky affair. In the dream, everyone was dressed in formal attire."

"What are you going to do?"

"I guess I need to tell Dana, but I don't think I should just call her. What would I say? 'Hey, Dana. Had a dream and saw Bill get killed.'"

I stared at him for a minute.

"You believe in my dreams?"

He glanced down at the tomatoes he was chopping.

"Not saying one way or another, but they do have an uncanny way of coming true."

He sounded annoyed as he said that.

"Drew, I heard Dana arguing with Bill yesterday. They didn't know I was there. I'd gotten there early. She sounded angrier than I've ever heard her in my entire life. She thinks he's cheating again. She told him she will kill him if she finds out he is."

"He doesn't exactly have the greatest track record, now does he?"

"No, but do you think she'd -" I paused. I couldn't imagine Dana hurting anyone.

"I've seen a lot of people do things they said they'd never do, babe," he said.

"I understand 'heat of the moment' more than I understand 'premeditated.' This looked premeditated. I can't explain that, but something about it seemed planned."

"Same here, but you don't know what Dana goes through on a daily basis. Bill is a narcissistic, egotistical SOB, and you know it. He's smart and controlling. And Dana left him once, so you know there's stuff going on that we don't have the details about."

I nodded. That made me feel even worse about abandoning our friendship.

The rest of breakfast was small talk about Emmie and the shop. He talked about a case he was working on, but there was another elephant in the room. There were things we needed to say, but we weren't. We had gone away a few months before and finally started reconnecting in our marriage, but it wasn't soon after returning that it all seemed to evaporate.

I took my time getting dressed. I wasn't sure how Dana would react or how I should tell her or if I should even say anything at all. I couldn't wait too long - I had to open the shop. I took a deep breath and headed to her house.

When I arrived, she was walking out the door to her car. She didn't have the baby with her. I pulled up to the curb and got out. She was standing in the driveway with a strange look on her face. She shook her head when I started walking to her.

"Hi Dana."

She stared briefly before she took a deep breath and started to glance around her.

"Something's wrong, isn't it?" her voice was breathy, and her eyes were wide.

"I need to tell you something."

"No. I don't want to know."

She started backing up and shaking her head at me. I thought she might turn and run at any moment. It was odd.

"Why are you acting this way, Dana?"

"You know something. You had a dream, didn't you? I can tell by that look on your face. I had a dream last night that you came to me to tell me about a dream you had. I don't remember the details, but it was bad. It was about Bill, and that he was - "

She stopped.

"He was dead," she said with a look of horror in her eyes.

She paused as tears welled in her eyes. Her stare bored through me. My face must've given her the answer she needed.

"I knew it. I woke up in a cold sweat. I begged Bill not to leave this morning, but he took Lily to my mother's for me to run some errands. I'm right; aren't I?"

I nodded.

"I had a dream Bill was killed. You were wearing a gold evening gown, and he was wearing a white sport coat and black tie and - "

"No, please stop. I don't want to know anymore."

The blood had drained from her face.

"Just because I dreamed it doesn't mean it has to happen. Sometimes it's a warning. Sometimes we can alter the details and change the outcome," I tried to convince her.

Dana was shaking.

"Trust me, Dana. I've had a couple of dreams about specific things and told the person. They changed something, so things couldn't happen like they did in the dream. Sometimes they are warning dreams."

She stared at me not seeming to believe me.

"Do you remember Jessica? I had a dream that she was on her way to work and that she died in a car accident. She changed the route she took and the next day she read a report of an 18-wheeler that jackknifed. No one was hurt, but it was the same spot she usually was at about that time every morning."

Dana nodded several times.

"Do you think the dream is about Friday?"

"I do. Can you change the party?"

"I'll talk to Bill."

She gave me a hug.

"Thank you, Grace."

I still had an uneasy feeling as I walked back to my car and headed to my shop. I wondered what it meant. I couldn't get the picture of Bill's face out of my mind. It was twisted and gnarled in pain as he touched his chest and fell to the floor. I wanted to shake it. I went to the back case and started thinking about some of the arrangements I had to make.

Around lunchtime, Dana appeared at the door. Her face was red, swollen, and tear-streaked.

"What's going on?"

"Bill won't listen to me. He thinks you're being vindictive and want to sabotage his plans for the candidacy. He thinks this is all a ploy."

I didn't answer right away. That didn't surprise me.

"What do you think, Dana?"

"I might've thought that if I didn't have that dream of my own. He won't listen to me, Grace. What am I going to do?"

"What if I talk to Drew about providing extra security?"

"I asked Bill, and he said this party is already costing too much. He's only going to use the minimum number of deputies required. He doesn't think we need those, but he's got to comply with city property. Besides, he wants to be mayor, so he needs to go by the book."

"Dana, who would want to kill your husband?"

She stared at me and shook her head.

"I don't know. I suppose a lot of people, to be quite honest with you. This doesn't have anything to do with your dream, but Grace, I think he's seeing someone."

I didn't tell her that I'd overheard their conversation a few days before, and I already knew this.

"Why?"

"I've seen a woman several times. She shows up when he and I are out, and she stares at us. I saw him looking at her one time. He said he didn't know her, but I could tell he was lying."

My first thought was Emmie and getting her to draw a sketch.

"How well could you describe her?"

Dana tilted her head at me and furrowed her brow.

"Emmie could get a sketch, and maybe we could get an ID and stalk her."

Dana's reaction was priceless. It was a mixed of confusion that ended with a spluttering laugh.

"Stalk her?"

"I think Drew would call it 'surveillance.'"

She laughed again.

"At least you're honest. It's worth a shot."

"Dana, I'll do everything I can to help you. I have a lot to make up for."

"Stop. I told you it was in the past, and when you're ready to finally meet Lily, we'll make that happen, too. I know you weren't ready today."

I sent a text to Emmie, and she agreed to meet Dana without Bill's knowledge.

It seemed to give Dana some reassurance. Emmie said she'd see if what she could do about using facial recognition software, but she didn't want to get in trouble with the FBI. Little else came from our conversations over the next few days as we prepared for the party.

Dana bought a new dress because she had planned to wear a gold one. I got a chill when she showed me a photo of it; it looked exactly like the one I saw her wearing in my dream. She even went so far as to take his white jacket to the cleaners and conveniently leave it there. He would wear a black tuxedo instead. I hoped her efforts were worth it, but the uneasy feeling wasn't leaving me. Dana asked if Drew would come to the party. She said she knew that Bill wasn't going to like the idea, but she would feel safer if we, or at least Drew, stayed. I did have a gun, but I'd never used it outside the firing range. That was something Drew insisted on, especially with me being alone in my shop sometimes. Besides, in the South, lots of women carry guns. It's not uncommon. But the one time I really needed my gun, I'd been knocked unconscious, so I didn't have a great track record of protecting anyone. I planned to just stay in the shadows and be there mainly as moral support for Dana.

3

My uneasy feeling continued when I picked up the newspaper on the day of the party.

There, on the front of the local news section, was a photo of Bill with his arms folded and leaning against the Haunted Pillar in downtown Augusta, and the headline to the story read "Businessman hints at run for mayor." The photo caption mentioned the pillar had brought him good luck in his life. His first date with his wife was in downtown Augusta, and their date included a walk to the pillar.

Most of us didn't really buy the legend of the curse that went along with the pillar, but we did find it amusing. It was a claim to fame for us since it had been featured in a cable television show about haunted places, and it was a popular spot to take photos. The truth was that the 10-foot-tall pillar was part of Augusta's lower market, which was destroyed by fire in 1829. The market was rebuilt, but it was destroyed again in 1878 in a freak storm that the historical marker at the site called a "cyclone." The lone remaining column was moved to the corner of Fifth and Broad streets.

Supposedly, the market was cursed by an itinerant preacher in the 1870s who wasn't allowed to preach near the market. He said anyone who tried to knock the pillar down would die. Despite living in Augusta all my life, I never knew anyone who had encountered the curse after touching the pillar, even though people swore it was true in that cable TV series. Everyone I knew had taken their photo at the pillar at some point in their life just to prove you could touch it and still live, and, yes, I'd touched the pillar and hadn't broken out with the plague. Still, it was a fun piece of history.

"He's really pushing his luck, isn't he?" Emmie was in stealth mode as she walked in. I was so immersed in the photo that I didn't hear her right away. I jumped when she started talking over my shoulder. She smiled.

"I don't know what I'd call him, Emmie. 'Pigheaded' comes to mind as well as a few other choice adjectives."

I laughed.

"You think?"

Emmie raised one eyebrow as she said that. She'd come in to help finish the arrangements for the party. She had put in a lot of time with the FBI lately, and they told her she needed to take some off. Her contract had only allowed for so many hours, and she'd exceeded them.

"He's ignoring your dream and Dana's. He's touching the pillar. And you do realize that today is Friday the 13th, right?"

"That had occurred to me, but I don't believe in the superstitions. The dreams, yes, but not the superstitions and certainly not the pillar curse."

"Well, I hope he's wearing his lucky boxer shorts or something."

I laughed.

"Like I said, I'm not superstitious. But he could've been practical. At the very least, he could've hired more security at this event. He refused. He even refused Drew's offer of free security."

"He told Drew 'no?'"

"Yes, he did, but Drew is planning on going anyway. Dana made him promise he'd be there. He agreed for her peace of mind."

Emmie went to the case and pulled out several stems. In dramatic fashion, she kissed one of the lilies and held it up as if in a toast.

"Here's to a long life, Bill. I only hope these aren't in your memory," she said.

"I hope so, Emmie. I hope so."

Emmie and I delivered the flowers ahead of time. Dana met us, wearing a pair of jeans and a T-shirt.

"No, this isn't what I'm wearing tonight, but there's a place I can change here. I couldn't ride back to the house and then be here in time."

"What did you decide to wear?"

She stared at me. Until that point, she'd had an uneasy smile on her face. I'd known her long enough to tell the difference between a real smile and the one she wore for beauty pageants. This one didn't even qualify for a half-hearted beauty queen smile. But when I asked about her dress, I thought she would burst into tears as her face twisted.

"The gold one," she choked out the words.

"I thought you bought another one?"

"Yes, but Bill made me return it. He has been really tight with money lately, and he said the gold one was beautiful. He wants me to wear it."

This wasn't looking good. I wanted to offer some encouragement, but the knot in the pit of my stomach wasn't going anywhere. It was only getting worse. I grabbed her hand and squeezed it, hoping to reassure her, but I couldn't reassure myself.

"Hon, let me help you fix your makeup," Emmie interjected. She was always good with supplying the right distraction at the right time. While she whisked Dana away to rescue her makeup, I put the flowers in place. The room didn't need much. It was already a beautiful space. With Emmie's bold, dramatic piece, everything was perfect.

The catering crew had taken over, placing chafing dishes for the heavy hors d'oeuvres and putting out the utensils, and the band was setting up its speakers and other equipment. And I could hear the usual train whistle in the distance. Downtown Augusta and trains would always be synonymous with one another in my book.

After bringing the smaller arrangements in, I checked on Emmie and Dana. Was there anything Emmie couldn't do? I wondered what she told Dana because she wasn't the same woman I'd seen a few minutes before. She had a real smile on her face, and her makeup was flawless.

The dress was stunning with its chiffon layers. It flowed over her curves and provided an elegant silhouette. Dana channeled the glamour of Hollywood yesteryear with the opera-length, white satin gloves. With her hair swept up into a French twist, she was gorgeous.

"Are you okay, Dana?"

She smiled and nodded.

"Emmie gave me a pep talk."

Emmie laughed.

"I told her I'd break her arms if she cried," Emmie said and winked.

I put my hands on my hips and tried not to laugh. How Emmie kept a straight face when she said it I wasn't sure.

"Really?"

"No, she convinced me that everything's going to be fine," Dana said and smiled a genuine smile.

I wasn't sure how she did that. Emmie always made me feel better; apparently, she was able to do it for everyone. It was definitely a gift I didn't have, so I was glad she was in my life.

As I stood there watching Dana in her beautiful evening gown, I felt completely underdressed. I'd worn a dress to work, but it wasn't fit for a black-tie event. When Drew arrived, he wouldn't be wearing a tux, either. I would have to stand in the corner in hopes of not being noticed. At least Emmie was as underdressed as I was.

"Your people await you, fair Lady Dana," said Emmie, giving her best curtsy.

Dana just laughed.

"Yes, it's getting close to that time, isn't it?"

"Yes, it is."

Emmie and I stood back as Dana headed into the party. It

wouldn't be long before guests started arriving. I was curious to see who'd been invited to this soiree.

"Shall we?" Emmie held out her arm for me.

I smiled and linked arms with her.

"I hope we are as happy at the end of the night, Emmie"

"Me too, sweetie. Me, too."

I really did love this venue even though the trains rattled the windows, and the train whistles often ruined the mood.

The guests milled in slowly. Emmie and I found a spot in the corner, where I hoped we wouldn't be noticed. I think she had other ideas because she liked social gatherings.

There was a small jazz band, but the singer had a microphone. He could compete with the noise of the trains. I guess I'd count trains since I really didn't want to be at this party. I was only staying to give Dana moral support, and Emmie stayed to give both of us moral support.

The flowers turned out beautifully. Emmie had outdone herself. They were majestic. She had an array of fall blooms, but it was the calla lilies that stole the show. She added an abundance of color, but the placement of the white lilies commanded people to look at them. She should be running this business, not me. I guess that's the reason I was the brains. I was adequate when it came to flowers. I could do pretty designs, but the ones that wowed people always belonged to her. Tonight, she truly wowed. She chalked it up to "pent-up creativity." I smiled because I was glad I'd asked for her help.

There were more people than Dana had told me were coming. I guess it was like a timeshare presentation. You know – they offer you some gift and in return you're pressured into vacation property. Except with this, Bill was offering free champagne and some incredible hors d'oeuvres in exchange for their votes. I think some people just came out of curiosity and to have something to gossip about.

Dana was the consummate hostess. She smiled and shook hands. Honestly, she looked like Grace Kelly, and she was as gracious as any princess ever could be. She was perfect for this role. She smiled and laughed. If I'd known better, I would've thought she was enjoying herself. I was not, except for listening to the jazz music. At times, though, it got a little loud, and I had to yell at Emmie to be heard.

When Drew arrived, he tried to take an inconspicuous spot in the corner with me, but Bill wasn't having any of that. Bill made his way through the crowd to Drew. He had to get close because of the noise.

"What are you doing here, Detective Ward?" he growled.

"Just performing my civic duty."

"I'm only tolerating her because of my wife," he looked at me when he said the pronoun "her." I knew that. I really wanted to leave. "I hired the correct number of deputies according to the law."

By now, Dana had reached his side.

"Bill, don't cause a scene," her voice hushed as she grabbed his arm. "Let them be. I'm the one who asked Drew to be here. It makes me feel better."

Bill glared at Dana as he shook his arm loose from her grasp.

"I told you to let me handle this. You're here to look beautiful and smile."

She hung her head for a split second. His words hurt me; I couldn't imagine how she felt. She was just the pretty face to him?

I could see Drew clenching his jaw, a sign he was restraining his anger.

"Why don't you stay outside, Ward?"

"Bill, please," Dana begged him.

A few people nearby began talking amongst themselves while looking our way. I was sure they couldn't hear, but they could see Bill and Drew weren't exactly happy. Bill saw them staring. He took a deep breath.

"Just stay out of my way, and we'll be fine."

"I'm only here because of your wife," Drew said.

Bill straightened his jacket and went to over to the two couples who'd seen the interchange. He was all smiles as he handed them champagne. Dana smiled, but it was back to the dull, fake smile she'd had earlier in the night.

Drew shook his head and turned to me.

"I have so many things I could be doing tonight, and this is not at the top of my list. I need to take a head count. I think this party is breaking the fire marshal occupancy code."

I could tell he was not happy. I wanted to calm the situation.

"The food is good, and I haven't had time to make dinner, so you might as well have some. Dana told me to help myself."

He grabbed a plate and milled around. I could see him watching everything that was taking place.

With the exception of the jazz band and the food, the party was a boring and stuffy kind of to-do. Of course, that was from my standpoint. I spent part of the evening counting the trains traveling through downtown Augusta. Their horns blared, and the building shook every time they went through. Emmie and I did enjoy seeing the women in their beautiful evening gowns. I guess that was the highlight for me, but I still wished I was home in my pajamas.

I suppose the other guests were having fun. They were smiling, talking amongst themselves - or yelling if they were standing next to the musicians. I think the champagne and hard liquor made it popular with many guests. I still couldn't figure the reason so many people had come to this shindig. I didn't understand Bill's appeal to anyone. I felt sorry for the city if this man got into the mayor's office. Maybe they just wanted to see the whole crash-and-burn process.

I kept my eyes on Dana, who grew increasingly worried-looking as the night progressed. She tried to stay close to Bill's side. I think he tried to break away from her several times during the night. There were tense glances between the two of them, and he tried to hide his anger. He didn't do a good job of it. I could tell he was aggravated with her. She was clingy.

I tried not to mingle, but there were a few people I did speak to, including Jimmy and Peggy Hughes. A lot of the others I'd seen in the paper, but I didn't know them.

"How's my favorite flower girl?" Jimmy asked as he gave me his usual peck on the cheek.

"I'm tired of yelling at Emmie," I yelled at Jimmy.

"What?" he asked and laughed.

Peggy smiled.

"He'll be coming to see you very soon," she said as she folded her arms against her chest.

He shrugged his shoulders.

"I'm always in the doghouse about something," he said and lifted his glass. "To doghouses, flowers, and making up."

He tried to give Peggy a kiss on the cheek after that, but she turned and walked away.

"I hope you have a lot of flowers ready because this one is going to cost me a lot. I mean a whole lot. I might need your entire refrigerator case," he winked before he walked after her.

"Peggy, darlin'," he called.

Emmie laughed.

"He will never learn, but that's good for you, Grace," she said.

"Maybe, but I can't imagine being upset with your spouse all the time."

Drew had come back in the corner with a large plate of hors d'oeuvres. They looked really good even though I wasn't sure exactly what they were. I usually ended up with a mouthful of crabmeat, and that was never good because I didn't particularly like crabmeat. Drew shook his head at Jimmy and Peggy as they left before shooting an annoyed glance at me. He wasn't happy to have been dragged into this.

Our corner of the room seemed to give us a good vantage point of the party. Although Bill avoided us for most of the night, he tossed plenty of dirty looks in this general direction. I really should have left the party long before. I probably shouldn't have been there after we finished decorating, but I was trying to support my friend. I should never have said anything about my dream because Bill was as alive and obnoxious as ever. Oh wait, I think that was actually his charming nature. The smarmy Bill was eating up all the attention. People fawned over him all night.

After he'd finished eating, Drew leaned against the wall with his hands in his pockets. His eyes never left Bill. Bill did duck out of the party a few times. Drew followed him and returned. Bill was never gone for more than five minutes at a time. Every time Bill left her side, Dana's cool façade dropped. I could see the fear as her shoulders weighed down.

The party dragged on. My feet were hurting in the heels I'd been wearing all day. I was ready for this nightmare to end. As the night lingered, Bill sauntered over to me in my corner. Dana followed close behind.

"Nice try, Grace, on ruining this party for me," Bill snarled as he took a swig of champagne.

"Andrews, you really don't want to make a scene in front of all these donors, do you?" Drew asked in a low, menacing tone.

Bill followed suit and lowered his voice as he moved in closer to us.

"She did try to ruin this night, and you can't protect her, Ward. She made up that whole dream thing to ruin this night and end my campaign. She tried to get Dana to cancel this event – all because I told her how I felt about how she'd treated my wife, who supposedly is her friend. All these people here love me. They wouldn't want to kill me. They know that I'd make a great mayor."

"Bill, you're drunk," said Dana.

I wanted to crawl into a hole.

"I'm just fine, Dana. Some friends you have. See, I'm perfectly fine. Everyone here has promised me their votes and their money for the campaign. It's a win-win all the way around. But stick around for a few more minutes. I'm going to officially announce my candidacy, and you'll see who my real friends are."

He sneered at me. I was used to people treating me like this over my dreams, but I couldn't handle it from him. He'd made me realize that I really wasn't a great friend to Dana. He'd already raked me over the coals more than once in the past few months. The tears had started to well up, and I rushed out of the building. The air was brisk, and I couldn't help but gasp for breath as I stood outside the door staring up at the moonlit sky. Drew was right behind me. He grabbed me and pulled me close.

"Babe, for once, I'd be so relieved you were wrong," he whispered into my ear.

He pulled back and looked at me.

"Bill Andrews is an arrogant -"

I cut him off before he could finish that thought.

"It's okay. Can we just go home now?"

"Whatever you want. We can even stop and buy some ice cream. That seems to be how Emmie cheers you up."

I tried to laugh.

"Thanks."

"Do you need to get anything from inside?"

"Just my purse. Emmie said she'd take care of everything else."

"I'll get it. You stay here."

After about 10 minutes, I began to wonder what had happened to Drew. It wasn't that big of a place. What could've kept him? I headed back into the building. The guests were still milling about. The jazz band was still playing. I didn't see Bill or Dana anywhere. I glanced around the room. I saw a couple of deputies. Drew was in the corner talking to our neighbor. She was having a dispute over a fence with the neighbor on the other side of her, and she wanted Drew to intervene. He'd explained to her before that there wasn't anything he could do, but she wouldn't hear any of it. I made my way to their corner, and I found my purse.

Drew was trying to get a word in edgewise, but every time he said something, she interrupted. It had progressed past the fence issue and gone into another problem with the neighbor's dog.

While she was talking to Drew, I decided to leave. Then I heard another train whistle. I guess I didn't need to be in too much of a hurry because I didn't feel like getting stuck by it or having to take an alternate route to miss it. Drew could be a while; our neighbor was never at a loss for words, and she never could get him at home. I remembered I'd left some supplies, and I'd have to pick them up on the way out. As I neared the storage room, I heard several blood-curdling screams from inside. My blood ran cold, and the knot that had recently left returned. I rushed into the room and found Dana kneeling over Bill, who was lying in a pool of blood. I could see the edges of the chiffon floating in the blood, soaking it up.

Drew pushed past me. I felt sick.

"Grace, call an ambulance. Dana, please move away."

My phone was still on the camera app after I had taken some pictures of the party. My fingers fumbled over all the apps, and I somehow managed to call 911. Then I pulled Dana close to me. Her face was ashen, and she was shaking. I grabbed her hand and squeezed it.

"Why wouldn't he listen?" she sobbed. I hugged her and held her.

"Maybe he's still alive, Dana. Hold on," I whispered.

She stepped back and shook her head.

"I want to," she choked out the words through her tears.

Paramedics were on the scene quickly, but I didn't think there was much hope. He was unconscious and had lost a lot of blood. Drew didn't speak, but his grim expression told me everything I needed to know. Bill was dead. Everything was a blur as the paramedics worked on Bill and put him on a gurney. Dana squeezed my hand as she watched their every move. She let go of my hand only to follow them to the ambulance. I walked outside and watched as they left.

Drew left me and went back into the main room. There had been quite a few people milling about even though it was obvious the party had been over for a while.

I realized I wasn't alone as Emmie touched me. She'd kept her distance while I was with Dana, but now her eyes were on me.

"Grace, are you okay?"

I glanced at her. I wasn't sure how to answer that question as her eyes penetrated me. My hands were trembling. I looked down and saw blood on them. I must've gotten it from Dana when I held onto her. The sick feeling wasn't passing. Other faces flashed across my mind. I could see the two previous murder victims I'd stumbled upon. Therapy had been helping. I wished I could go back. How could I ever get all the blood and Dana's horrified face out of my memory?

"I don't know, Emmie."

I choked the words out. I didn't know if I was going to cry or throw up. I felt light-headed. I thought after two murders, I'd get used to this. I was wrong. I couldn't breathe even in the fresh night air.

"Was he dead, Grace?"

"Pretty sure he was."

I was numb. I didn't want to be right this time. I wanted my dreams about Mark and Linda to be the last time I dreamed about someone I knew dying. As I stood there, the dreams about the two of them flooded back. It was almost a year since I had the last dream of Mark shooting his wife. Well, I didn't see Mark shooting his wife or himself. I'm thankful for that part. I only saw glimpses of them, and I just knew. Sometimes, you knew things in the dream with no explanation or with no one speaking. You simply knew, and Drew never told me the details. Maybe, deep down, I really didn't want to know.

I'm not sure how long we stood and stared in silence. The ambulance was long gone, but I guess we didn't know what else to do. Drew returned and touched my arm, breaking me out of the daze I was in.

"Babe, I have to make sure someone questions you about what you saw once again," Drew said. "After you give your statement, you don't need to be here. Emmie, you're going to have to be questioned, too. Then, would you mind taking Grace to your house?"

"I don't mind at all," Emmie answered for me. I said nothing

- just stared into the distance. I hated it when people talked about me as though I wasn't even in the room. I took a breath.

"Drew, you don't have to send me to Emmie's house. It's not like this is the first murder scene I've been to."

Drew narrowed his eyes at me and tightened his jaw. He wasn't happy, but then again, in the past few months, he hadn't been happy with me much at all. He put on a good show for everyone in public, but that's not how he always was in private. Sometimes, he was fine, the old Drew I knew. Most of the time, though, he was a stranger - an angry stranger.

"Grace, you're not a detective, and this scene is much worse than the last two."

I felt like I was 4 again as he turned and walked away.

"What's his problem?"

Emmie folded her arms across her chest and her eyes followed him as he headed back to the building.

"The anniversary of Mark and Linda's deaths is next week, and he's really been on edge lately."

"He's never talked to you about that, has he?"

"It's the elephant in the room, and he refuses to deal with it, Emmie."

"So, this isn't about your being on the scene; this is about your dreams?" she sounded confused.

"Not really my dreams, but the details of what went on that night continue to haunt him. It scares me. I know how he's tried to deal with the pain."

"I thought he was going to counseling."

"He had been for a while, but he stopped. He doesn't think I know. He was different when he was talking to someone. He was happier. He seemed like he wasn't as stressed out."

"Is he drinking again?"

I hung my head without giving a verbal answer.

"Oh Grace, I'm so sorry," she gave me a hug. "This is definitely a chocolate chip cookie dough ice cream night with chocolate syrup and maybe even some chocolate chip cookies on top."

I tried to smile. She linked her arm in mine.

"Let me give my statement to Mr. Personality, and we'll go."

"Maybe we should go to the hospital?"

"It's possible Dana will need someone, Grace."

"Yes, but will she blame me?"

"Did you do whatever happened to Bill?"

"No."

"Then why do you blame yourself, Grace?"

"Drew blames me for Mark and Linda."

I tried to brush away the tears that were beginning to fall.

"I don't think he blames you for Mark and Linda. I mean, you didn't kill them, either."

She paused for a minute and smiled.

"If you want, I can set him straight," she whispered in my ear.

I pulled away and didn't respond. I knew she was trying to get me to smile. I didn't want to have these dreams. Why me? What good did it do? They didn't save Bill; they didn't save Mark and Linda.

"Let's go give our accounts of tonight and then leave," Emmie said.

"That's fine."

I rattled off what I'd seen and heard to one of the deputies. When I was released, I walked around the parking lot until I found my vehicle and leaned against it. I wasn't worried about standing outside late at night. By now, there was a battalion of sheriff's deputies swarming the place. I felt defeated. My husband was still angry at me for something that wasn't my fault, and I'd already let my childhood friend, Dana, down after the birth of her baby. Now this. I was glad Emmie was still talking to me.

I felt something vibrate in my hand. I'd been holding my phone this whole time without even realizing it. It was a text from Dana.

I can't believe he's gone.

I sank down to the asphalt. As much as I disliked Bill, I didn't want this to happen. Dana was probably better off without him, but I certainly wasn't going to be the one to tell her that. He was her husband - for better or worse - although I'd felt she'd gotten more worse than better. And she'd held him in her arms as he died. I had a ton of questions, but I hated text conversations.

Do you need me to come to you?

As I waited for her response, I heard voices behind me. Since I'd slid to the ground between two parked cars, I was hidden from view.

"Can you believe the nerve of that Bill Andrews? Who would vote for him for mayor anyway? Whoever did this did Augusta a huge favor. We've had enough shady characters in our government."

Wow. So much for respect for the dead. Not that I would've voted for him. I'm sure he would have done what he could to finagle the votes, though. I couldn't recall voter fraud claims in Augusta despite shady politicians.

"He had so many enemies in this town. I don't know how he survived this long," came the reply as I heard a car door shut.

I wondered who would kill Bill Andrews at a public event. Of course, it was done in private area where no one could see them. There were still a lot of people around; surely, there was a witness.

I stared at my phone hoping to hear from Dana, but a text from Drew popped up. He wanted to know where I was. In a few moments, he arrived.   He helped me up from the ground and pulled me close to him.

"I need you to tell me what you saw."

"I heard screaming after that train whistle stopped blaring. It was the longest train whistle of the night. I found Dana kneeling next to Bill's body. They were both covered in blood, and she touched me. Now I have Bill's blood on me."

I looked at him.

"Do you think - " I paused. We were standing underneath a street light, and I could see Drew's facial expression. He raised an eyebrow. That look told me everything I needed to know. Dana was at the top of the suspect list.

"Do I think what?"

Of course, that would be your answer, Drew. You're not going to give anything away.

"Dana?"

"Babe, leave this to us."

"She's my friend."

"I know. That's why you just need to step back from this and let me do my job. Go to Emmie's. Take a shower. Eat ice cream. Pray. Cry. You do what you need to do, and I'll handle my part."

His response was brusque and dismissive.

I started to say something when Emmie walked up behind me.

"Have you given your statement, Emmie?" he asked.

"Yes, I've been excused, and I am ready for death by chocolate."

"It's going to be a long night, Grace. Enjoy your girls' night with Emmie."

He pulled me into his arms and held me. I wanted to think this was sincere, but I felt it was a show for Emmie. Why did I think these things? I rested my head against his chest. I knew he loved what he did, but I hated his job at times. And this was definitely one of those times. I hated all the time it took from us, and I hated the situations it put him in. And the stress he was under, I hated that. Now, we were dealing with friends and in light of the anniversary, I was concerned. No, I think scared out of my mind was more accurate. I was more afraid now than I'd been when I was kidnapped a few months back. I prayed hard. He kissed me on the top of my head and let me go.

"I'll call or text you, okay?"

I nodded and watched as he headed back into the building.

"Have you heard from Dana?" Emmie asked after Drew was out of ear shot.

"She sent me a text saying Bill was gone. I asked her if we

should come to her, but she hasn't responded."

"I'm not sure what we should do. You know that's got to be where Drew is headed next, and he won't like it much if he finds you there."

"Yes, I know. He's already taken care of babysitting arrangements, hasn't he?"

"You really are on edge, sweetie. Let's get us some chocolate. Dana is probably surrounded by family right now. She probably doesn't need us."

"You're right. Her parents are probably with her. And as for chocolate, I want chocolate ice cream, peanut butter cups, chocolate chip cookies and chocolate syrup."

"Wow, I was just joking on the death by chocolate thing, you know."

I tried to laugh as I got in my car.

"I'll meet you in the frozen food aisle, Emmie."

4

I didn't want to go to Emmie's. I wanted to go home and crash in my own bed. It had been a long day. I wasn't sure I could sleep, though. I just wanted to be alone; it wasn't like I expected Drew home any time soon. Emmie's boys were with their dad, and we always enjoyed our slumber parties. Emmie had so much more personality than I did. I wasn't sure why she wanted to hang around me. Anyway, we went back to being 16 on the nights we spent together. It was nice to feel like a teenager again.

Jazzy worked on Saturdays. She was scheduled to open the shop in the morning, so at least I didn't have to worry about being there first thing.

I changed out of my dress into some yoga pants and T-shirt and threw it in the washer, I scrubbed my hands of Bill's blood, but I felt like Lady Macbeth. I still felt like I had his blood on my hands – in more ways than one.

"Did you find out anything about that mystery woman Dana mentioned?"

We piled scoops of ice cream and crumbled chocolate chip cookies and peanut butter cups into bowls. No one was counting calories tonight. This was emotional eating at its best - or worst, depending on your point of view. I tried to rationalize the eating because I hadn't eaten much all week - not since I had the dream about Bill.

"No, I still haven't heard anything. Someone is running facial recognition on her. I hope we get a hit."

Emmie walked to her couch and sat with her legs folded under her. She pulled out her phone and sent a couple of texts.

"Emmie, you don't think that Dana -"

"Killed Bill?"

She finished my sentence when I paused. I nodded.

"Dana is too refined to kill anyone, but I wouldn't blame her if she had. Do you know how he was killed?"

"I didn't ask Drew. Not that he would tell me anything. But it's it always a gunshot, isn't it? That's always the easiest and quickest."

"Wow, you have gotten cynical."

"You think?"

Emmie nodded.

"It's been a hard year."

"I know, honey. I know," she said.

Putting her spoon in her bowl, she reached for my hand and gently squeezed it before going back to the decadent confection.

"Well, I don't think too many people are going to miss him, sad to say. We know he was slime. I can't really even think of a word to describe him," she said.

I paused before I said anything.

"I heard Dana and Bill fighting a couple of days ago when I met them to talk about the party. She threatened him. It's all surreal now. Her threatening him and then finding her next to him in a pool of blood."

"Stop. I'm eating ice cream, remember?"

She was right. I wasn't hungry any longer. I put the bowl and spoon down.

"If she did kill him, and I seriously doubt she did, who could blame her?"

"Would a jury see that, though?" I asked.

"I'm sure there are plenty of people who could testify to what a louse he was."

"I wonder how many of them would be interested in killing him."

"I bet we could make a list," she suggested.

"You're probably right. I'm sure I could be on that list."

Emmie looked at her phone.

Her name is Sunny Kim. My FBI sources are helping me with information."

I was confused with her abrupt shift in the conversation.

"What are you talking about?"

"The sketch I made of the mystery woman. Facial recognition came back. It's a woman named Sunny Kim, and she owns Osana Spa," she read off the screen without looking up at me. "Or at least she did until she was busted a couple of years ago."

Sunny Kim. The name sounded familiar.

Emmie smiled and raised an eyebrow.

"You remember? It was all over the paper and TV news."

"Oh, that spa."

Emmie nodded.

"Yes, the one and the same, where they were giving more than massages."

"You got it."

"She served six months and got out. Now, she is the manager for another spa called Happy Massage, but ownership is in the name of - "

Emmie stopped and shook her head.

"What?"

"William A. Andrews."

"Seriously?"

"Yes."

"I wonder what happened there."

"I'm sure it's a lead, but I don't think I'll bother Mr. Personality right now."

I tried to laugh.

"Is that your new nickname for Drew?"

"He seems really stressed out right now."

I nodded.

She put her ice cream on the table and went over to her desk, pulling out a notebook and pen.

"We'll do this the old-fashioned way."

"Are you sure that notebook has enough paper to list all the suspects?"

Emmie laughed and put her hands on her hips.

"Grace Ward, I'm surprised at you."

"We both know it's the truth."

"Sadly, I think you're right."

Despite the talk of pools of blood, we managed to eat our sinfully rich desserts as we tried to come up with suspects and scenarios for the murder. It sounded like the premise from a popular board game - How did Bill end up in the utility room in a puddle of blood?

It didn't take long before we were exhausted. I think we pretty much named everyone in Augusta, including Emmie and me. I had a motive, plus I had means. Drew made sure I had a gun in my purse at all times. But I didn't have the opportunity, did I?

"I'm so tired, Emmie, and I have to work tomorrow."

I got up and put my shoes on to leave.

"It's after 2. I thought you were just going to crash here."

"No, that was what Drew wanted. I want to go home. Thanks, though."

"Suit yourself."

A knot formed in my stomach, and I hesitated.

"Listen, don't go to sleep right away."

"Okay. Why?"

"In case I decide to come back."

"Why would you come back?"

I shrugged my shoulders.

"If Drew isn't there, I might want to come back."

She nodded, but she was eyeing me. She didn't believe me.

The drive wasn't a long one, especially at 2 in the morning. There weren't many cars on the roads.

Drew's car was out front when I arrived, but all the lights were off. The only light in the room was from the television. The screen door squeaked as I opened it. I tried not to make too much noise as I stepped into the room, but the hardwood floor wasn't cooperative. It creaked with every step I took. Not that it mattered. Drew didn't hear me, couldn't hear me. I can't say what I saw surprised me. Disappointed me, yes, but no surprise. Drew was sprawled out on the couch. He was still dressed from his day minus his tie; his shirt was partially unbuttoned, and his sleeves were rolled to three-quarters. I saw an empty bottle on the floor beside him. The floor seemed to get louder the closer I got to Drew, and the smell of alcohol grew stronger with every step. I picked up the bottle carelessly thrown on the floor and the glass that was tossed on its side. Had he drunk the whole thing? Yes, the amber-color bottle was dry, and I noticed another bottle on the table. I didn't touch it. I didn't want to know if it was empty. Since I didn't drink, I had no idea just how much he would have to consume before ending up in a state like that. A knife twisted in my heart. This was the reason he wanted me to go to Emmie's. He didn't want me to know what I had suspected. I was pretty sure he'd been drinking and hiding it. Now, I knew. Most nights, he just came to bed later than I did despite my pleading for him to join me earlier. He probably drank then. At least, that's what I always guessed. I never found empty bottles. I think he tried to hide them from me, but I had a feeling this was what he did every night.

I knew this month would be hard for him, but without getting him to talk to me, there was nothing I could do to help him. I stood looking at his face. He was out cold. I wasn't sure what I felt. I was angry, but more than that, I had a deep hole inside me knowing he was turning to alcohol instead of trying to face his demons and get rid of them. Why wouldn't he talk to me? Why wouldn't he let me into that dark part of him? I was his wife. For better, for worse. I promised I'd be there for the worst.

All those thoughts of being a failure began to flood me once again. After all this time together, he still couldn't confide in me, trust me with his feelings, lean on me. Or was it just male ego that caused him to keep his feelings bottled up? I thought we had made headway that morning six months ago when he threw the coffee pot to the floor, and I threatened to leave. But the subject never came back up even though I tried. The tears coursed down my cheeks. I didn't want to wake him. At this point, though, I wasn't sure I could wake him. I knew he didn't want me to see him like this. I hated secrets. I placed the bottle and glass back on the floor where I'd found them. He started to stir, and I backed away.

I pretended I was 16 earlier when spending time with Emmie. Now like that teenage me, I wanted to run away. I sent Emmie a text to let her know I'd be back. I cried all the way back to her house. I'm sure my eyes were red and puffy. I felt like a teenager past curfew when I walked to the door to find her waiting for me. I knew she was staring at me, but I couldn't look at her. I didn't say anything. I just shook my head. I tried to walk into her room. She had a giant king-size bed, and she didn't mind me taking a corner of it. But she grabbed me first and gave me a big bear hug.

"When you're ready to talk, I'm here for you."

"I know, Emmie, I know. I just feel like I've talked and talked, and it's done no one any good."

"I'm sorry I haven't been here to help carry the load."

"Emmie, I never wanted you to."

"Friends make the world an easier place to live in."

"I know. I love him, but I'm afraid for my marriage. Lately, he's been angry. He's one way around other people, but at home, he's so different."

"I thought you had a breakthrough at the beach after the ballerina died."

"It only lasted a couple of weeks."

I shook my head.

"I can't, Emmie. Not now."

I couldn't sleep. Too many thoughts; too many emotions. Maybe it was a good thing we didn't have children. I wouldn't want them to see their dad struggling this way. Maybe this was a blessing in disguise. I don't know if I'd be a good single mom. Single mom. I'm not sure where that came from. I still wanted to be married to Drew, but not this way. Something had to change. Something had to give. I wasn't sure how much more I had to give if he wasn't going to at least try to meet me halfway.

Around 6 a.m., I decided I couldn't lie awake any longer, so I dressed and headed to the Savannah River. At some point, I had to check on Dana. I didn't think it would be a great idea so early in the morning. She'd never texted me back last night, and I was getting concerned. I also wondered about Sunny Kim. I did an Internet search on my phone and found the articles about her and her spa, which was allegedly a front for a prostitution ring. She was found guilty and went to jail, but apparently, she was back in business with a partner. I wonder what his death meant to her business. I doubt she could get the proper licenses to keep it running.

I found a park bench and faced North Augusta. I angled myself to watch the sun rise over the Savannah River as a hazy mist hovered above the water line. The sky, painted in its majestic palette of brilliant yellows and oranges, put things in perspective sometimes. It was going to be a beautiful day - at least, weather-wise. Despite the rich colors of the sunrise, I felt gray.

I stared across the river at the beautiful homes on the other side. I wondered what problems they faced. Did they face the same ones I did? I needed to find a way off my own troubles and onto someone else's, I supposed.

I drifted from thought to thought. I glanced at the leaves, which still were a rich green despite the October date on the calendar. Of course, fall didn't really come here until around Thanksgiving. The leaves fell when they wanted. My parents had an oak that typically lost its leaves in January and was bare only a few weeks before the spring awakened it to new life. I knew my thoughts were random; some of them didn't make any sense; others had to do with my grocery list. Finally, I looked at my phone, and it was 8:30. I wasn't sure where the time had gone. I was so into my thoughts. I sent another text to Dana. I wanted to know how she was. That was relative, of course, since her husband had just been killed. And she found the body.

I didn't wait for a response as I headed to the flower shop to find Jimmy Hughes standing outside my door waiting on me. For me, it meant a paycheck, but it didn't look good for Jimmy.

"How's my girl this morning?" Jimmy asked as he gave me a peck on the cheek while I tried to open the door.

"I'm hanging in there. I was expecting you after last night. It must be pretty bad this time."

"Bad isn't the word for it. I'm in water deep enough to float Noah's ark, if you know what I mean."

"Poker game, Mr. Jimmy?"

"Much worse than that, I'm afraid. I loaned Bill Andrews some money for a business venture, and well - I hate to say this since he's not even in the ground yet - I don't think I'll get that back. Peggy was counting on that money to buy an addition to the beach house and an around-the-world cruise or something. I don't know. Even with flowers, I'm going to be spending a lot of time with our pet schnauzer."

"Ouch."

"Ouch is right. I love Dana, but this was a gentlemen's agreement. No paper trail."

"Had you given Bill money before?"

"A couple of times when he was younger. Believe it or not, he always paid back with interest on time. I know what people have said about him, but some of it simply isn't true."

"So, what are you here for today, Jimmy?"

"Well, I need you to ease the pain."

I laughed.

"That sounds like you might be in a doghouse we can't get

you out of."

"We can always get Jimmy out of the doghouse," Emmie interjected. She'd used her key to come in the back entrance without my knowledge.

"Peggy can always tell when Emmie designed the flowers. No offense, Grace."

"None taken."

"Make it bright, splashy, and really, really big so she can put it on the dining room table. You know that thing seats 16 people, so it needs to take up the middle and be the first thing she sees when she walks into the dining room," he said. "Money is no object. Well, it is, but you know what I mean."

"Make it look expensive?" Emmie asked.

"Definitely. How soon can you do that?"

"I'll have to see what flowers Grace has available."

"I'm stocked."

"Then, give me an hour."

He nodded and left the store.

"So, are you going to tell me why you came back and left so early this morning?" Emmie asked.

"No sense in talking about something I have no control over. Did you hear why Jimmy was in the doghouse?"

"Yes, I did. I heard most of the conversation. Just because Drew is shutting you out doesn't mean you have to shut me out."

I glanced up at her and nodded. She could read me better than anyone. I shrugged my shoulders.

"He was passed out on the couch with an empty bottle of whiskey on the floor and another bottle of something else on the coffee table. That's the reason he insisted I go home with you. He didn't want me to know, and he wanted to drink in peace, I suppose. Any other questions?"

"Nope, I think that about covers it. I'm sorry, Grace."

"It's not your fault. Back to Jimmy then? Do you think there was some bad blood he wasn't telling us about?"

"Anything is possible."

She glanced at her phone and looked up.

"Have you heard from Dana?"

"No. I want to go over there. I'd love to show her the photo of Sunny Kim to see if that's the woman who she said has been stalking them."

"Same here. You said Jazzy is coming in, right?"

"I'm here," said a perky voice behind us. "Sorry, I'm running late. I know I never do. Beth's kids kept me up all night playing video games."

Emmie headed toward the back to find flowers for Peggy's arrangement, and I watched her as she pulled out the flowers I had left over from Bill's party. I had ordered too many. I guess that had been a good thing. She used some of the mums and added roses and carnations and those amazing calla lilies.

"Did you get these gladioli from Mr. Tompkins?"

"Of course, I wanted something special for Bill's party, and Mr. Tompkins' greenhouse is a treasure trove. I love getting a chance to go there. It's rare."

"I know," she said and laughed. "How did you get in?"

"Well, he lets me in every now and then, especially when I need something out of season and fast. He also has the unusual and exotic. He helped me with some of those rare orchids for Alexsandra. He has a sweet spot for Mama's lemon cake. Mama helps me out when I'm in a jam. He had some beautiful colors in there."

"Your mom's lemon cake," Emmie laughed. "She could bribe me with it any time."

She looked through the stems.

"You aren't kidding me on the colors. These are amazing. Just how big is his greenhouse?"

"Greenhouse? You mean greenhouses, don't you?"

"True. You've only told me about one."

"Well, he has a few and so many different flowering plants. I'm not sure what his secret is. I think he lives in the greenhouses."

"This will be beautiful, and I think Peggy will love it."
She smiled.

"Thanks. I needed some creativity, Grace. I'm starting to feel like me again."

"Do you think I should just go over to Dana's? I don't know what to do. I've already let her down so many times over the past year. She needs someone."

"I think you should stay away from Dana for a few days."

The sound of Drew's voice gave me chills and not good ones.

I turned around to see him walking through the shop into our work area. He had bags under his eyes. He hadn't shaved this morning. I tried not to stare at him and turned quickly back towards Emmie.

"Have you talked to her, Drew?" Emmie asked.

"Not yet," he directed that comment to Emmie before turning his attention to me. "You need to stay out of this."

"She's my friend."

"You've kept your distance from her for almost a year. You need to do it now."

"Are you telling me that as a husband or as a cop?"

He raised an eyebrow at me.

"Don't get involved in my investigation, Grace."

That had an ominous ring to it and was given in a low-pitched tone I knew too well.

Emmie put down her shears. She picked up her phone and walked over to Drew.

"Well, it's too late for that, Drew. We have a couple of leads for you," Emmie's voice was like ice.

She showed him the photo of Sunny Kim and filled him in on Bill's business ventures with the woman previously convicted on prostitution and solicitation charges.

"And if you also need another place to look, try Jimmy Hughes, who apparently is in the doghouse majorly for investing money into Bill Andrews, but you didn't hear that one from me.

You'll have to figure another source for that."

Drew stared through Emmie to me.

"I came to see how you were, Grace."

His tone was still confrontational, so I wasn't sure what to make of the question.

"I never thought I'd say that I'm get used to seeing dead bodies, but I guess I am. I'm just concerned about Dana is all. She won't return my texts."

"She collapsed last night and is supposed to be at home in bed. Apparently, she's expecting again, and all the stress isn't exactly good for her."

"So soon after Lily?"

Drew nodded. He moved toward me and placed one hand on my arm.

"What did Dana say happened last night?"

Why was my first thought that the only reason he came to see me was to get information? Didn't he just say it was his case and for me to butt out?

"I didn't really talk to her. I told the deputy last night that she said she found him. Why are you asking me again?"

He just looked at me.

"Did you find a weapon, Drew?"

He narrowed his eyes at me.

"My case, Grace."

I glanced at his hand on my arm, and he let me go. I couldn't tell what he was thinking as his eyes ran over me.

"It's going to be another long day today. I'm not sure when I'll be home. If you're not okay and need to stay with Emmie, I understand."

I didn't answer, and when he leaned in to give me a kiss, I turned my head away. He kissed my cheek and stepped back. He didn't say that because he cared about me and my mental health. He said it because he didn't want me home. I felt like he was cheating on me with bottles of whiskey and his job. Crazy thought. Maybe,

maybe not.

"I'll call you later."

I nodded again.

I was seething as he left the shop. I folded my arms against my chest as I replayed his words. I wasn't sure what made me more angry - his secrets or his wanting to control my every movement. Don't come home; don't see Dana; don't get in the middle of my investigation. Sorry, Drew, but once again, I'm there - whether you like it or not.

"Emmie, I'm not spending the night at your house tonight."

"Yes, ma'am," she replied as the words I'd spoken came out much harsher than I'd imagined.

I took a deep breath and turned around to see Emmie staring at me.

"So, when are you going to Dana's?"

I laughed.

"Why? Do you want to go with me?"

"You know it. You know I'm nosy and helping you with two murders put this bug in me. Being around the FBI has made it even worse. I don't know what I'll do for excitement when this contract is up," she paused and laughed. "Yes, I know I'm full of contradictions. On the one hand, it's hard. It's sad. It's brutal. But on the other hand, it gets your adrenaline going even if you're not the one chasing the bad guys."

I had to take a few deep breaths. Drew had upset me more than I realized when he told me to stay away from Dana.

"Grace, are you okay?"

I shrugged my shoulders.

"Is that how he is now?"

"Yes, a lot of the time."

I sent Dana another text to see how she was doing, and to my surprise, this time she responded. She was still in the hospital. They'd kept her overnight. With her history of miscarriages, they were watching her closely. I knew she'd been running herself ragged even though she had looked fine to me, glowing even. She said doctors gave her some fluids because she was dehydrated, but she would love a visit.

With that, I pulled out a vase and some richly colored blooms and started working on an arrangement. Emmie eyed me.

"What are you doing, Grace?"

"Mama told me that I should always take something when I'm visiting someone in the hospital."

"You do know you are going to incur the wrath of Drew, don't you?"

"You know what? I don't care. Maybe, just maybe, if I can push the right button I can get him to open up and spill everything he's kept inside."

"Maybe so, sweetie, but explosions of any kind can be dangerous and deadly. Think volcanoes and bombs."

"I know, Emmie, but I love him. He can't keep all this inside forever. The drinking and secrets aren't helping him. He's been taking money out of the accounts. I'm pretty sure I know where the money has been going. This will kill him if he doesn't stop."

"I hope you know what you're doing. I'm here for whatever that's worth."

"Thanks, Emmie."

It didn't take long to finish a cheerful arrangement, but I wasn't sure it would cheer her. I mean, her husband just died in her arms. I did feel I owed it to her to visit her despite what Drew said. I had guilt that I would never be able to get rid of. One act of penance wasn't enough.

5

Jimmy Hughes had asked for a big arrangement, which meant there was no way he could transport it without damaging it. With Jazzy staffing the shop, Emmie and I loaded up the arrangement. Dana's could be held as we drove.

We stopped at Peggy's house first. It was on the South Carolina side of the Savannah River not far from the Interstate. It was perched high above the river, overlooking it with a stunning view. I had been in her home only a few times, but I loved to gaze out her windows which formed the back wall of the house. It was breathtaking, especially if you were afraid of heights. Depending on the angle, it looked as though you could open the door and fall down the rocks into the river. That was an illusion, of course. There was plenty of space between the house and the edge of the steep hill that was dotted with trees. I often wondered what a sunset might look like through those windows. It would have to be majestic. I had admired the changing leaves in the fall plenty of times as I drove across the nearby I-20 bridge but looking down over them must've been magnificent.

Peggy met us at the door. Everything about Peggy was perfect. Her hair was set each week during her appointment with her hairdresser. It was a platinum blonde to mask the white hairs that naturally grew. Her nails were manicured to a perfect red that mirrored her lipstick. She shook her head and placed her hands on her hips when she saw us unloading the massive arrangement.

"That Jimmy is a rascal," she said and laughed. We joined in.

"I'll just need to replace anything that might have gotten damaged," Emmie said as Peggy threw open the walnut doors. The home had light maple floors, and the decor was a mix of traditional and contemporary. She was proud of the antique pieces passed down from her mother and grandmother, but other rooms showed her eclectic personality. She had an array of fun, colorful pieces of artwork created by some of Augusta's many talented artists.

After we put the arrangement on the table, Emmie moved toward the art wall in the living room. With her mouth open, she stared at the many pieces arranged in a hodge-podge pattern.

"Peggy, do you have anything new?" Emmie asked.

"Oh, Emmie, I know you appreciate my art," she said. Her angry demeanor began to melt. "Come over here and let me show you."

Emmie followed her closely while I stood back and listened.

"This one is by Marion Ivey. He's a folk and metal artist, and he uses recycled items. Someone I know has a painting he did on a washing machine lid."

She moved over and pointed an outdoor scene with lots of bright colors.

"This one is from Staci Swider. She incorporates a lot of texture in her works. She was a textile artist at one time. I love how she adds texture in her nature prints. That's what I like about hers - rich colors, rich textures. It draws you into the work."

She moved to a painting inspired by the black box theater downtown. It featured a black cat in silhouette.

"Now, I had a hard time getting the artist to part with this one," she said. "He's a little shy. His name is Chris LaMantia, and he's a great actor. He can do physical comedy better than anyone I've seen in Augusta. But he also paints. He did this one for one of the plays downtown."

Next to that one was a brilliantly colored sketch. It looked like some sort of fairy, and the colors were amazing.

"This is Sarah Pacetti. She does a lot of what people might call comic book art, but she calls it sequential art. My granddaughter really liked something she saw Sarah do so I decided to get this one for me. "

She pointed once again.

"And Jay Jacobs. He is one of my favorites. As you can see, I have several by him. He cuts wood and paints it, and you never know what he's going to come up with. He's also done some pieces inspired by The Beatles and David Bowie."

Listening to Peggy was fascinating, but I was chomping at the bit to get out of there to talk to Dana. I wished Emmie would hurry up even though I knew she was interested in Augusta's art scene. Emmie was drinking it all in. She seemed entranced by each piece and couldn't remove her eyes from them.

"And last but not least, this one I got last week. It's by Erica Pastecki."

It was a whimsical 1950s vintage inspired painting of a woman wearing pearls and an apron. To the side, there was a seamstress's dummy wearing an identical apron.

"Erica is such a hoot. This one is called 'Just Because I Want A New Apron Doesn't Mean I Can Cook,'" Peggy said and laughed.

That title drew giggles from all of us.

"She does a lot of these. She calls them The Apron Series, and they all have those sarcastic titles," she said.

I stood back and stared at the amazing variety of art on her one wall. I loved that Peggy didn't mind that they didn't match. They were various sizes, painted in different types of materials, and on widely different subject matter. Individually they were amazing, but as a whole, the art wall was gorgeous.

"Peggy, you are an artist's dream. You love our stuff and put it out for everyone to see. Thank you so much."

"I'd rather pay a living artist than buy something out of some big-box store. And I'd rather have art than guns or knives. I just wish

Jimmy felt the same. He's got a collection of guns and knives in the basement in his man cave. Oh, my goodness," she said.

She paused for a minute and then pointed at Emmie.

"And Emmie, I need one of yours."

"A gun or knife?" Emmie asked.

"No, silly girl. Your artwork. I heard about you being a sketch artist so that means you've got to be super-talented."

"Of course, I'm trying to twist Grace's arm into letting me have a show," Emmie said and giggled. She winked at me.

"Oh Grace, you need to."

"Actually, Peggy, it's been Grace's idea for a long time. She's been doing the arm twisting."

"Well, if you have one, I'll be there, and I'll buy the first one. If you are half as good of a painter as you are a floral designer, there's no question that it will be fabulous."

"It's nice to have a fan," Emmie answered.

Peggy laughed. Her initial aggravation had now faded. She was her regular self.

"And the flowers, they are just perfect."

"Well, Jimmy wanted 'big, bold, and splashy.'"

Peggy sighed.

"Jimmy has a good heart, but he lets people take advantage of that goodness sometimes."

"We love Jimmy, but we hate that he comes to see us so much. Well, we hate the reasons he comes to see us," I interjected.

"Oh, he's so full of it sometimes. I'm sure he makes me out to be some kind of horrible wife, but that's not the case at all. I just watch things closer than he does. He'd spend all of our money or give it away to Bill Andrews. I shouldn't talk especially since the man was family and was brutally murdered practically in front of both of you last night. But I know my husband. He can't keep a secret, and if he had you bring me that gorgeous arrangement then I know he told you why I was upset," she said.

I nodded.

"Did he tell you he loaned Bill $100,000?"

"No, he didn't."

"One. Hundred. Thousand. Dollars."

Peggy punched every decimal of the amount.

The conversation was becoming more interesting now. Maybe this was Emmie's plan all along - to lower Peggy's guard so she'd start talking. Jimmy never talked bad about anyone. He was a happy-go-lucky kind of guy, and he was very trusting. I knew from the fact that he just gave me his credit card number without even asking for a price.

"Anyway, he loaned it to him about four months ago, but I didn't find out until a couple of days ago, when I needed to take some money out of our account to make a payment on something. It was gone. Bill was supposed to start paying it back - or so Jimmy said. Now, we'll never get it back."

"I'm sorry, Peggy," said Emmie.

"Did he borrow it for his mayoral campaign?" I was curious now.

"No, it was for some business, but to be honest with you, I think Bill had borrowed money from the wrong people to begin with or even gambled it away. I think they came back to settle the score."

"Loan sharks?"

"I don't know if that's what you'd call them. There are always dangerous people. And Bill was mixed up in all kinds of things. We always knew that, didn't we? Jimmy feels like he owes Bill because Jimmy's mom and Bill's grandmother were sisters. With Bill's parents gone, Jimmy feels like he has to watch over Bill. He was close to the Blakes at one time, but I think he burned them."

The Blakes.

I swallowed. That was a name I hadn't thought about in a long time.

"The Blakes?"

"Yes, Harper Blake is Jimmy's cousin. She took him in in a way, and he and Trevor were close as young boys. I think Bill tried to

56

cozy back up to them recently. Harper has cancer. Bill makes sure that Dana takes Lily over there on a regular basis. I love Dana, but how she got involved with Bill is beyond me."

I'd often wondered the same thing.

"Jimmy's right. I've been upset over this money thing. Bill's had shady dealings. And from what Jimmy told me, Bill was into some heavy gambling and a lot of gambling debt. I just hope that he didn't drag my Jimmy down into something, too. Now, Jimmy is going to have to dig deep into that antique gun collection of his to pay for this one."

"Jimmy's guns are antiques?"

"Oh, yes. His man cave is downstairs in the basement. He has a Revolutionary War musket and a couple from the Civil War. Plus, some swords. Goodness, I have no idea what's down there, but he might be able to start his own war with those things. I just hope no hoodlums ever find out about it."

"Do you have any idea who might've killed him?"

"Grace, you're starting to sound like your husband."

She sounded flustered as she said that. I bit my lip. I wasn't sure if that was a compliment.

"I did have to talk to Drew last night, you know. The whole thing was horrible."

"Yes, it was horrible."

In my mind, I could see the image of Dana and the blood on her dress. Her expression was terrifying. A wave of nausea swept over me.

"Did you find him, Grace?"

Finding dead people seemed to be a newly discovered talent or something. It certainly wasn't one I wanted.

"Sort of. I heard Dana screaming, and I was close to where the screaming was coming from, so I was in the room before anyone else arrived."

Peggy seemed agitated. She began wringing her hands, and her eyes darted between Emmie and me.

"I did hear people talking at the party last night that there had been a big blowout between Bill and someone before the party started. You know rumors, though. I heard several different names. Who do you believe? But I'm not sorry he's dead – not in the least. I do have plenty of theories, though, and I shared them with Drew."

I was surprised to hear Peggy talk that way. She was opinionated and headstrong, and she never let anyone stand in her way, but I didn't think she'd hurt anyone. Never mind that thought. Peggy always got what she wanted. I'd heard that Jimmy had been engaged to someone else before Peggy came in and stole him away.

"Grace, you have to tell Drew. Jimmy is a lot of things, but he's not a murderer. He wouldn't kill anyone, even if there was $100,000 involved."

That was an odd statement. I wondered why she made it. It wasn't like we were accusing her husband of murder, and if he killed Bill, he wouldn't get his $100,000 back. I couldn't stop my brain from going all the places it was going. I still wanted to help Drew solve this despite his adamant resistance. Then as though the murder had never happened, Peggy switched back into hostess mode and started chatting with Emmie.

"Emmie, you've outdone yourself on that arrangement. I'm sorry I didn't say anything when you first brought it in. It's absolutely gorgeous. Now I need to have some company, so they can see it."

So much for talking about last night. I wondered if she was hiding something. She did a radical 180. Peggy smiled as she talked about the flower arrangement. Her eyes started to sparkle. That was the reason I loved flowers and art so much. They both had the power to uplift people and change their moods. And in some small way, maybe I did something to make people's lives better, although I couldn't take the credit for Peggy's mood change. That was Emmie's doing. Sometimes, I was jealous of Emmie. She was so much better with people than I was, and she was so much more creative than me.

The conversation steered toward flowers with no more mention of Bill Andrews. To make sure we'd fulfilled all our social duties, we stayed about more 10 minutes after Emmie finished freshening up the arrangement.

It didn't take Emmie long to start talking once we'd gotten in the van.

"Well, she is full of information, isn't she?"

"All she needed to do was tell us about Bill's affair with Sunny Kim, and we might've had it all put together."

"Peggy mentioned the Blakes. I haven't heard that name in a long time. They keep pretty much to themselves."

That name used to have a lot of meaning for me.

"Grace, you know Trevor Blake was at the party last night, right?"

I kept my hands on the wheel and looked straight ahead.

"Really? I didn't see him. I kept my eyes on Dana most of the night."

"Yes. I saw him a couple of times looking in your direction."

"And that's supposed to mean something, Emmie?"

I shot her a glance and turned the radio on to stop her from talking.

6

Dana had texted that she had been discharged from the hospital but to please stop by her house instead. When we arrived, we rang the bell and got a text response to come in. The door was open.

I carried the flower arrangement back to the master bedroom. Dana was in bed and was surrounded with folders and papers.

"Don't get up."

I'd noticed Dana trying to gather all the papers up and move. She'd done some redecorating since the last time I'd been inside her house. Her bedroom was perfect. Everything was in white - all the coverings, pillows, and sheets. She had pops of color in the room. There were a couple of matching flower paintings over the bed, a stark contrast to Peggy's eclectic mixture of art. They were abstract swaths of red with dabs of green, purple and blue.

"Are those for me?" she asked, pointing at the arrangement I held in my hand.

"Of course. I'll just put them down on the bedside table."

She nodded.

"Thank you."

"What are you doing?"

"I'm trying to see what kind of mess Bill left me in."

"Where's Lily?" Emmie asked.

"She's with my mother."

I sat down on the edge of the bed. Dana was wearing a pair

of sweat pants and a t-shirt. Her eyes were red and puffy. There was a box of tissues on the bed and a small trash can on the floor that was full of used ones.

"Are you - "

"Pregnant?" she answered my question without me finishing.

"No. I was going to ask if you were okay, but that's probably a stupid question."

"I haven't been 'okay' in a very long time, Grace. Longer than you know. And yes. I have a six-month-old, and I am pregnant for right now, but I've been so stressed out planning this party. I overdid it. I was supposed to be resting, taking care of myself, and I'd been spotting most of the week, now -"

She couldn't finish the sentence. She didn't cry at first.

My heart broke for her. I knew too well what she was going through. The feeling that all the tears you had were used up. You felt empty inside.

"I'm going to be a single mom. I never thought -"

She broke down into tears and covered her face with her hands. I put my hand on her shoulder. Emmie joined me on the California king- size bed that practically needed a stepladder to get on. She reached out for Dana's hands.

"I don't know what I'm going to do," she said. "We have so many debts. I had no idea, and I don't even know what half of this is."

She shook her head.

"There seem to be no insurance policies, just mountains of debts and bills."

"Dana, you should rest. You don't need anything that would stress you out any more than you already are."

"I have a funeral to plan. I don't know how much that's going to cost. I need a life insurance policy to pay for it. What am I going to do?"

She placed her hands over her face and began to cry.

I reached for the papers and started making stacks. Emmie

followed me and moved things away. Dana took her hands away from her face. The motion seemed to have startled her. Dana's jaw dropped, and her eyes darted from me to Emmie.

"What are you doing? No, don't. I don't want you to see how bad things were. Please."

She reached for the papers and tried to snatch them from my hands. Her aggression surprised me.

"It's okay," I said as I pried them from her hands and stacked them. "I'm going to take them into the other room. Doesn't Bill have an office?"

She nodded, but I could see fear in her eyes. I wondered exactly what was in this stack of papers I was holding.

"Out of sight, out of mind. Okay?"

"You, young lady, are going to rest," Emmie sounded like she was talking to her boys as she pushed Dana back into the pillows.

"But I -" Dana tried to protest.

"Look, Grace and I both know this spiel. They've sent Bill's body to the crime lab for an autopsy so no body, no funeral yet. There's no law that says you have to bury someone two days after they've died. I'm not sure where that custom came from. You can take longer to plan this, and you can take today at least to rest and probably tomorrow, too. And you need it. We can tell."

Dana nodded her head and started to weep. Emmie slid closer and pulled her close to rock her like a small child as Dana cried. I just watched the scene play out, and my feelings of helplessness increased. Why didn't Bill listen to me? A pregnant wife and infant left behind. And what was up with the insurance? Surely, he had taken care of that. Once out of Dana's sight, I thumbed through the papers; only one insurance policy. I thought Dana said there wasn't one. I was confused. Maybe she just overlooked it. I pulled it out and glanced over it. It was for $1 million, and the beneficiary wasn't Dana and Lily; it was Jimmy Hughes. Now I was really confused. Why was there an insurance policy with Jimmy Hughes name on it, and who had taken it out, and what was it doing in Dana's stack of papers? Something else caught my attention. It was a brown envelope. I opened the envelope and out slid photos of Jimmy Hughes and a very young, partially unclothed woman. I thought I might be sick. Did I say very young? She was extremely young. I guess she could've been 18, and I really hoped she was at least 18. I wondered about the "loan" now.

None of this made any sense to me. I put the papers down on Bill's desk and started to head back into Dana's room when I heard the doorbell. I thought I'd have more time to see Dana and leave before Drew got here. I should've known that I'd probably run into Drew here, and he wasn't going to be happy with me. I knew I couldn't hide. He'd already seen my delivery van outside. He knew I was there. I took a deep breath and went to the front door to open it. Drew was there with another deputy.

He narrowed his eyes at me and motioned for the other deputy to move to the other side of the room.

"Grace, not the person I came to see, but I do need to talk to you," he said.

I nodded. I admit I was nervous. I swallowed.

"I'm sorry, Drew," I started.

"What have you found out since earlier this morning, Grace?"

I stared at him. He didn't seem angry, just direct and efficient. He was on the job. Right now, it wasn't my husband standing in front of me. It was a homicide investigator trying to solve a case. His right eye twitched. This was getting to him. And to me. I shrugged my shoulders.

"You're asking for my help?"

"I don't have much choice, now do I?"

He folded his arms against his chest. I couldn't tell if he was angry or not. I was looking for his gritted jaw, but it wasn't there.

"I know you've been snooping, and I want to know what I'm going into," he said.

"Well, when we got here Dana was going through these papers. They were hugely in debt. Peggy told us that Jimmy loaned

Bill $100,000, and I saw this insurance policy in these papers. Jimmy Hughes is the beneficiary of a large insurance policy taken out on Bill two weeks ago."

Drew pursed his lips and nodded.

"The insurance policy is for $1 million. And there are photos in here of Jimmy and some very young woman. Also, Dana doesn't know if he left her anything but debt. And one of the businesses Bill was involved in was a massage parlor. That woman that Dana said was stalking them, the one she thinks he was having an affair with used to own Osana Spa."

I was talking at the speed of light. Something that tended to happen when I got nervous. My hands were shaking as I searched for the photos of the papers on my phone. I held the phone out to him.

"These are in a folder in Bill's office. So much for Jimmy giving Bill a loan. Sounds more like something else."

He looked at the photos and shook his head.

"Hush money?" he asked. "Blackmail is a good reason to kill someone. Peggy Hughes would kill Jimmy if she saw these, or she'd at least put him in the poor house forever and make his life miserable."

"I think that's an understatement."

"And it appears that Sunny Kim is back to old tricks," he said.

"Your guess is probably better than mine," I responded.

"I'm sure she was. She had quite a client list, and she was pretty bold about it. I doubt she was having an affair with Bill in that sense of the word. For her, it would've been all business. She would want payment for any services rendered."

"I don't want to hear that, Drew."

"Maybe not, babe, but it's the truth."

"I guess you were familiar with that other case."

"She'd proposition anyone she thought would do business with her, but her list of potential business partners was pretty slim given her history."

"You aren't angry with me?"

He looked at me for a minute.

"For coming to see Dana, you mean?"

I nodded.

"I knew you'd come here, but there are some things you're getting ready to find out that I don't think you want to know."

"You mean more than I already have?"

"I know things, and Dana will probably say some things you don't want to hear. It's going to hurt, and you're really going to hate yourself if you stay."

That sounded ominous. Great.

"I'm saying that to you as my wife. You believe the good in people. That's a great thing, and it's one of the reasons I fell in love with you. But you have to realize people aren't always what they seem."

"I know. Do you think she –"

"Anyone at that party last night is a suspect."

"Me?"

"I ruled you out, but you did have motive and opportunity. And you own a gun, don't you?"

"You know I do."

"Don't worry, Grace. I won't be putting any cuffs on you. Not here anyway," he smiled and winked at me.

For a minute, he was the old Drew that I knew. He could be a riddle at times. In his profession, he was intense and driven, but the Drew I'd always known had such a playful and light-hearted side to him. And the real Drew came out at the most unusual times, like now in the middle of all the tension and pain.

I couldn't help but smile at him. He always knew how to get me to drop my guard, but it was so rare for him to make jokes lately. His mood swings were getting to me. I didn't know this man most of the time. I felt like I was walking a mine field when I was around him.

"Thank you for your help. I just don't want you getting in danger again. I don't know what Bill was involved in, but I have a feeling he was a small fish in a big pond. Things could come back to you, and I want to do everything in my power to protect you."

"What are you talking about?"

"Everything you just told me shows me there's more to this than meets the eye. It's my job to keep you safe, and I didn't do that a couple of months ago. I have to do that now. You have to understand that."

"Drew, so it was a gunshot?"

"Looked like a gunshot, but the autopsy will tell us."

"Did anyone hear anything?"

He shook his head.

"No one claims to have heard anything, and I didn't either. There was a train that came through minutes before I heard Dana screaming, plus the crowd noises and the musicians. That could've drowned out the noise from a shot. significantly. The window was open in that storage room, but Dana said she didn't see anyone leave thought it."

"I counted trains last night. It was a busy one, and that last whistle was a long one, almost like someone was on the tracks and they were trying to get them to move. That last train was a slow one. I remember thinking that because I didn't want to get caught by it."

He nodded.

"Drew, Peggy said Jimmy has a huge gun and knife collection too. It's making Jimmy look bad isn't it?"

"Doesn't help his case out right now. People came and went quickly, and the lights at the service entry weren't working last night. It was dark on that side of the building."

"Do you have any other leads?"

He nodded, but he looked at me with a raised eyebrow.

"My case, Grace. Please back out."

"I know, but I thought you wanted my help."

"I did, and you gave it to me. Now you're asking questions. Several people said they saw Bill arguing with someone before the party started."

"Really? Do I know them?"

"You aren't going to give up, are you?"

"No, I'm not."

"If you or Emmie find out anything else, please call me."

"I will."

He stared at me for a moment.

"I'm giving you the chance to leave now."

He didn't wait for my response, but turned and walked toward Dana's room, where he knocked on the door. I kept my distance, but I did follow him into the room.

"I'll only talk about this with them here," Dana said.

Drew nodded.

"Dana, we have to ask you a few questions. We'd like to do that alone."

"Please, Drew. Please don't make them leave. This has been one of the hardest weeks of my life, and I need them here. I begged them to come because I knew you'd be here," she said.

He pursed his lips and glanced at the other deputy who was with him.

"This is Deputy Graham," he said. "We got everyone's statement last night and yours, but there are a couple of things I need to ask."

"Unless you're here to arrest me, anything you ask can be done in front of my friends."

She said that but then stole quick glances at both Emmie and me. I could see fear written across her face. What did she have to be afraid of?

"What was your relationship like with your husband?"

She shook her head.

"I don't understand why you're asking that."

"I just need to how things were between the two of you."

"Fine. We were like most married couples, I suppose."

"Dana, did your husband have affairs?"

She gasped as though she wasn't expecting that. She shook her head frantically as she seemed to struggle for words.

"Why would you ask me that?"

"Just answer 'yes' or 'no.'"

Drew was firm, matter-of-fact. His voice was void of emotion. Dana hung her head as she grasped Emmie's hand.

"Yes," she whispered without looking up.

"Was he having an affair when he died?"

"I don't know," she choked the words out. "I think so."

"Dana, did you threaten him?"

Her head jerked up to look at him.

"That lying, evil - " she bit her lip to stop herself. I could tell she was trying to hold back her tears. "Yes, I'd threatened him, but Drew Ward, I – I didn't murder him. I told you last night that I heard him talking to someone before I found him. I couldn't tell who. The noise of the trains and the band. I wasn't sure."

Drew didn't bat an eyelash.

"Dana, did he abuse you?"

That was the final straw apparently as Dana slumped over on Emmie and began crying uncontrollably. I was totally useless. I stared at Drew, and his glance told me all I needed to know. We'd been married long enough for me to read his expression that said this was the reason he didn't want me here. I stared at the white duvet. Dana continued to cry without answering Drew's question.

"Dana Andrews, was your husband abusive?"

She nodded and pulled back from Emmie and locked eyes with Drew.

"You know the answer to that question, Drew. Don't you?"

His face still lacked any signs of expression. He stared at her waiting for her answer.

"Yes, my husband was a horrible man at times, but I didn't murder him, Drew," she pleaded with him. "Believe me, there were times that I thought about divorce, but - "

Her head dropped, and her shoulders heaved as she sobbed. Emmie threw her arms around her and gave Drew a poisonous glance.

Drew didn't answer. I wondered if he was going to arrest her. After all, she did have means and plenty of motive. But was Dana capable of murder? I stood up and moved to the window. Who was I kidding? I wasn't there to comfort Dana. I was there because I wanted to be in the middle of all of this. I wasn't sure what happened to me since that first murder case. I was different. Sure, part of me wanted to be involved with Drew's work so I could help people - mainly him - but I wasn't sure I liked the person I was becoming. My heart was getting calloused. I felt all sorts of anger toward Bill and to Drew. What happened to the girl who loved flowers and just wanted to make people smile? This was the darkness I saw in Drew as well. The darkness Drew drank to forget.

"Dana, don't go anywhere. We aren't done here."

Drew's voice was hard and sharp. His words penetrated me. I wondered what they did to her. She didn't look up but simply sobbed against Emmie's chest.

Drew turned to leave the room without looking at me. I understood why he didn't want me there.

Dana sobbed for several minutes.

"I didn't want you to know the things Bill did."

Her eyes were red and puffy. She glanced at me.

"Did Drew rake you over the coals before he came in? You were gone a while," she asked.

"Not too badly."

Dana tilted her head.

"Are things okay between you and Drew?"

I didn't know how to answer that, so I didn't. I resorted to the classic game of "Grace changes the subject."

"We're here to check on you, Dana, not me."

She glanced at me then at Emmie.

"You were telling us about Bill," Emmie interjected. She and I were good at this game. Emmie knew I didn't want to answer Dana's question.

"Okay. Well, when I was pregnant the first time and when

Lily was born, he acted like a different man toward me," Dana started to cry again.

Emmie handed her another tissue.

"He had been kinder, gentler. He'd changed, or at least, he seemed to," Dana's speech was choppy as she fought against the tears. She gulped for breaths as she tried to form her sentences.

"When he found out I was pregnant again, he was overjoyed – we were overjoyed. We couldn't believe we could have another baby. Lily was such an overdue miracle. Bill's done nothing but shower me with gifts. But something wasn't right. I began having doubts that this could really be permanent. The gifts seemed to be a diversion from –
"

Dana cried harder and didn't speak for several moments. It was painful for me to see her this way. She deserved better than all of this. She was a good woman. She raised money for charities, especially organizations for children. She volunteered so much in the community, giving of herself and her time.

She took a deep breath as she went on.

"In the past couple of weeks, he seemed distant, pre-occupied. He gave me presents, but he wasn't into it," she said. "Gifts were always a smokescreen when -"

She put her hands over her face for a few moments.

"When he was having affairs."

"We found out who that woman was," Emmie whispered. "He owned a business that she ran."

Dana tilted her head to the side slightly and furrowed her brow.

"What are you talking about?"

"Emmie drew a sketch and facial recognition software came up with a hit. The woman owned a massage parlor a couple of years ago and served time on prostitution charges. She is the manager of a business in Bill's name."

Dana shook her head.

"Bill owns a massage parlor?"

She put her hands over her face and began to cry again.

"I can't deal with any more of this today. I just need to rest."

"I'm sorry. We came here to comfort you and have done the opposite."

"It's not the two of you. I appreciate you being here when Drew came to talk to me."

"Do you mind if I ask you one more question?"

I had to find out who this person was that Bill argued with. Dana nodded.

"You said you heard arguing before you found Bill. Did Bill argue with anyone before the party?"

The blood drained out of Dana's face.

"He was upset with Ray at one point."

"Ray? Who's Ray?"

"Ray Finch. He promised to be Bill's campaign manager. He's a real estate agent, and they've done several deals together. He's good with people and numbers."

"Do you know what they were arguing about?"

"Bill said we'd talk about it later. I didn't see Ray for a while. I think he left and came back because I did see him near the end of the party."

Dana took a deep breath.

"Do you think it might've been Ray who was arguing with him," she paused. "Maybe he was there before I found Bill."

Dana seemed to be digesting the information. She didn't look as scared as she did earlier.

"I didn't want to be alone, but now, I think I need to be alone."

"Please call me if you need anything, Dana. I wasn't here for you before, but I want to be here for you now."

"Thank you, Grace. You have helped me. You just don't realize it."

We both gave her hugs before walking out the bedroom.

Too many thoughts were going through my mind as we

walked out of Dana's house. It seems we had lined up several suspects for Drew. Dana had reason to kill Bill but so did both Peggy and Jimmy, although I couldn't imagine any of them as killers. I wondered about Sunny. If she'd been stalking Bill, was she hiding at the party? Did she kill him there? I hoped that one of my first three choices was off. Then there was Ray; that was a new player in the game. But we really didn't know anything about him. I wasn't even sure I knew who he was.

I remembered Jimmy telling me he had an appointment at 1, and it was just after noon as we left Dana's house. Our visits had taken less time than I'd thought. I had a hunch, but I had to ditch my van and get a personal vehicle, so I wouldn't be spotted.

"It looks like Jimmy, Peggy, and Dana all have a motive. I wonder about Ray. Maybe we should find out more info on him," I said as we waited at a traffic light.

"Still trying to solve this one, Grace?"

"Oh, come on, Emmie. You actually want me to believe you're not?"

She laughed.

"Well, of course, I am. Now that's I've worked for the FBI, stuff like this is even more in my veins."

"I think it's always been in our veins. Do you remember spying on that couple's house when you thought your ex was having an affair?"

Emmie laughed.

"Oh, my goodness. I'd forgotten about that, and we went to the wrong house."

"How could you forget falling in the holly bushes while trying to get a closer look, and it was two people in their 90s?"

"I thought for sure we were going to jail that night. They were getting ready to call the cops."

"Fortunately, we only had scrapes and bruised egos. You managed to talk them down."

"Yes, Drew and his 'you're busted for breaking curfew' look

when you came back with your clothes dirty and the sleeve on your shirt torn where it got caught in the chain link fence we were trying to climb over. I thought he'd break up this friendship for good on that day, and I don't envy your teenage daughter one day."

I laughed at that one. Drew did have a look that could strike terror in the heart of anyone. I guess that's why he was so good at what he did.

"I'm just glad that we didn't find your ex cheating on you."

"We both knew he was. He confessed to it. But you're right. I didn't need to find the proof."

"Drew's not the only one who has tried to break us up. That's just like our teacher trying to separate us in third grade. Remember the case of the missing pencil? We were convinced someone stole your pencil with that eraser in the shape of some character. I can't even remember what character it was, but it was from some cartoon we watched."

"Oh wow, Grace, the missing pencil. I still think it was the kid with the glasses. He loved that cartoon and talked about it all the time. Yeah, you've been my partner in crime for a long time, so what's our next move?"

"I think we have a lead to follow."

I popped inside my shop for a few minutes to make sure Jazzy had everything under control.

"Anything exciting, Jazzy?"

"Well, not really. It's just a typical college football Saturday, which means it's pretty dead in here. Since all the teams are playing this weekend, there aren't any weddings. You people take this college football way too seriously."

I just laughed.

"Yes, there are definitely people who take it seriously, and don't you forget it. I just love the condolence bouquets that the Bennett and Squires families send each other."

"Well, I'm learning."

The Bennetts and Squires were families joined in marriage,

but they were feuding in-laws when it came to college football.
On one side were the Bennetts, who all went to the University of
Georgia, while the Squires' clan all went to the University of South
Carolina. When one Bennett married a Squire, the house was divided
on Saturdays in the fall. Depending on who won that game, one
of the families would be getting a funeral arrangement in the best
assortment of Georgia red or Carolina garnet. The winning team
would send their colors to the loser. And both families got a laugh,
well usually. It was the only time I ever delivered anything on a
Sunday, but Jazzy had volunteered to be the bearer of bad news this
year.

"Let's go, Emmie."

"We just came in."

"I have a hunch."

We got in my car. It was getting close to 1 p.m.

"I think I know where I'm going but look up the address to
Happy Massage or whatever she calls it now."

"Are you serious?"

It was only about 10 minutes away. I wondered if Drew had
made it there yet. It was in a former house that had been converted
into a business. We could park across the street. There was a fast food
restaurant, and we probably could hide in the crowd. I went through
the drive-through and pulled into a space, so we could eat our lunch.
This reminded me of all the stake-outs I'd watched in movies. Emmie
and I did have some adventures. I certainly didn't need to be seen,
and I hoped Drew wasn't in the area.

"What are we looking for, Grace?"

"Not what but who."

Our timing was perfect because within a few minutes, I saw
exactly what I was looking for. Jimmy Hughes pulled up and went
inside.

I pulled out my phone and tried to snap some photos.
Emmie's jaw dropped.

"Was that your hunch, Grace?"

"Yep."

What was Jimmy mixed up in? He'd been my parents' friend; he'd been my best customer. I thought I knew him. I was having a hard time believing all of this. I sat with my eyes on the building. It was getting hot in the car even though it was October. I rolled the windows down. I had to think out loud.

"So, a couple of months ago, we found out Bill had a thing for prostitutes when we were in the middle of the human trafficking ring case. Now we learn Bill is behind what may or may not be a front for prostitution given who operates the business in his name."

I pulled out my phone and found the photos of Jimmy and the young woman. I handed my phone to Emmie. Her mouth dropped as she scrolled through them.

"Jimmy supposedly loaned Bill money, but these photos make me think Bill was blackmailing Jimmy. Plus, there's an insurance policy with Jimmy as the beneficiary. Dana has been abused and humiliated by this man who we all have hated."

"I can't believe Jimmy would do this," Emmie said as she viewed the photos.

"Neither can I."

"Peggy must not know about that insurance policy in Jimmy's name."

"I don't know. We can pin it on a lot of people right now, but we both know Bill had lots of enemies. It could be practically anyone. For all we know, it was some random homeless person off the street who came in looking for food."

"All that is true. I just don't see how it could be any of them. I mean, these are people we know, Grace."

I stared at my phone. What was I going to do with this information? My husband was mad at me. I guess I'd be mad at him, too, if he was coming into my shop and trying to arrange flowers. I laughed out loud at the thought. Emmie narrowed her eyes at me and shook her head.

"What?"

"I was imagining Drew arranging flowers."

Emmie giggled.

"That would be a sight."

Jimmy wasn't in the building for long. He came out with Sunny following close behind him. Her arms flailed around her as she spoke to him. Actually, I was pretty sure she was yelling, considering she pointed at him several times. I recorded this on my phone. I wasn't sure if it was coming out or not. I wondered what she was saying. Oh, to be closer. When he reached his car, he turned around. She was tiny. She couldn't have been 5 feet tall, if that. He towered over her, and she cowered away from him. He stood there until she went back inside the building, and then he left.

"I wish I had super hearing or could read lips," Emmie said.

"No kidding."

I sat there trying to figure out what to do next. We had nothing on Sunny.

"I wonder if Jimmy has a connection to the spa."

Emmie picked up her phone and typed something into it.

"I wonder if my FBI friends can help."

"Why?"

"Do you think any of this could be related to Jillian's sex trafficking ring that we learned about in April?"

"Why do you say that?" I asked

"Well, she was in Augusta and bringing girls through. Maybe there's a connection. I mean it was a pandering charge that got Sunny in trouble before."

"Yes, but Dana thought they were having an affair."

"Sex and money. He seemed to like to mix the two."

"I wonder what Jimmy was doing there."

Emmie glared at me.

"What?"

"I don't think you want to know the answer to that question, Grace."

"Maybe I don't, but if Jimmy knew about Bill's business

dealings with Sunny he could be trying to get a cut of the action – or the business. You know – to get the money back."

"Are you forgetting about the insurance policy? That's pretty suspicious, don't you think?'

"True, but I'd love to be a fly on the wall."

"You aren't kidding. Well, I think we're done in. Somehow I don't think you and I are the type of clients they are looking for."

"So, what's our next move?"

"I have no idea," I said. "I don't know much about Ray what's-his-name. I guess we could stalk him, too. He's the only one on our list; otherwise I'm out of guesses unless something pans out from your text to the FBI."

"Ray Finch – the fixer. He's supposed to fix Bill's image, but did you see Dana's face when we asked her about the argument?"

I nodded.

"She looked almost relieved. It was strange. She was terrified up until that point."

"You're right, Grace. It was weird."

"I've been meaning to ask you. Didn't Drew set you up with Butch from the sheriff's department?"

"I wouldn't say it that way. He introduced us sort of. We went out a couple of times, but I see what you go through being married to Drew. And this job with the FBI has been so stressful, I haven't had time to date anyone. He still calls, but I'm trying not to hurt his feelings. I'm enjoying being Emmie – single and happy."

"I guess that's a good place to be."

7

I tried to wait up for Drew. I hadn't heard from him all day. He usually called or texted or stopped by the shop during the day. Nothing since our meeting at Dana's. I had so many things I wanted to talk to him about - and not just Bill's murder.

I stayed in the living room, but I fell asleep on the couch. It was a vivid dream as most of them were. Drew and I were at the lake. He was in a playful mood, splashing me with water and threatening to pick me up and throw me in. He chased me out of the lake and onto the shore. I tried to run, but I was laughing so hard, I couldn't. Besides, who can run in the slimy red Georgia clay that is in some spots at Clarks Hill? Not that it really mattered. I wanted him to catch me. He pulled me in his arms and held me close. I looked in his eyes, and he smiled before his lips met mine in a deep passionate kiss.

Then he pulled back. He winked at me, giving me his mischievous grin before throwing me over his shoulder. I protested, but he just laughed. He headed back into the water and dunked me beneath. When I came up, I couldn't see him anywhere. I looked around and called his name. Then I saw his head bounce above the water before he was taken under again. Was it a current? How was he drowning? Drew was a strong swimmer. But I couldn't reach him. I screamed his name. He called back to me. "Grace, help me" before he went under again.

The image of him calling my name and gulping the air as he

went under the muddy water was the last thing I remembered before being jolted awake. I was out of breath as I sat up on the couch, and my heart pounded in my chest. I gasped for air. Too vivid, too real, too true. I was trying to save him in the dream, but I couldn't. And that's what I had been trying to do in reality for months – save him from himself.

It took a few minutes for my eyes to adjust to the darkness. I reached out for my phone. It was 2:42 a.m. And I had no missed calls or texts. I stood up and headed to the bedroom, but Drew wasn't there either. I peeked out the front window. No car. If something had happened to Drew, someone would've come by or called me. I sat back on the couch, wondering what to do. I knew I didn't need to worry about his physical well-being, but I did anyway. I thought about texting Emmie. I didn't want to wake her. I'd been determined to come home. I wondered why he was so late. I didn't have to wonder long as I heard a car pull up in the driveway. I sat in the dark and waited for him to come inside. He tried to open the door without much noise.

"It's okay. I'm awake."

The clank of keys hitting the table was the immediate response.

"I thought you were going to Emmie's."

He was gruff. No, "hey, babe, I missed you."

"I never said I was going to Emmie's. I live here."

I turned on the light. He winced. He came to the couch and sat down next to me. He ran his fingers through his hair and leaned his elbows on his knees. This wasn't a good sign. He wanted to tell me something, but he didn't know how. I knew this pose all too well. I'd only seen it a few times, so it made a mark on me because usually what followed was painful. The dream had caused my heart to start sinking, and now, it slipped even more.

"I'm going to stay at Butch's house for a couple of days."

"Why?"

"This isn't working."

His words punched through me. I couldn't breathe.

"What?"

I was surprised that I could say anything. The word stuck in my throat.

"Us."

I couldn't say a word. I knew we were going through a rough patch, but I thought we'd work through it. We'd always worked things out.

"You and me. We aren't working anymore."

How did someone respond to an opening statement like that? And where did it come from? I knew he was having a hard time, but never in my life did I imagine those words coming from him. He needed space from me? We weren't working? Maybe I wasn't awake yet. Maybe I was still dreaming. This couldn't be happening.

"I'm sorry about Dana. She asked us to come be with her. She needed -"

"This doesn't have anything to do with you being at Dana's. I've talked to a lawyer."

"A lawyer?"

Surely, I hadn't woken up yet. He just sat there hunched over with his elbows touching his knees.

"I can't do any of this anymore, Grace. I used to be able to keep my professional life separate from our personal life. I had a work box and a home box and a box for us. Now all the walls are down. No more boxes. I can't do this anymore, and I can't protect you."

"Please, Drew, don't say that."

I could feel the tears streaming down my cheeks. I knelt in front of him and touched his hands.

"Drew, I love you. I have always loved you. Please stop shutting me out."

"This isn't about you loving me. I can't do this anymore, Grace."

Throughout the whole conversation, he'd focused on the floor boards. He wouldn't look at me. When he finally raised his head,

I saw the tears on his face. I touched his cheek. I moved closer to him and kissed him. I'm not sure I'd ever kissed him this way. It was a mix of passion, fear, and desperation. At first, he didn't respond. He almost acted surprised. He pulled back from me and stared. But then he responded with as much emotion as I'd given him. I still loved him, and I believe he still loved me. Surely, our love was enough to get us through. He picked me up and carried me to our room. There were no words; only raw emotions, but throughout it all, he never looked at me, even when he kissed me. He kept his eyes closed. I often thought you closed your eyes while kissing to savor every feeling, but I wondered if he closed his eyes so I couldn't see into them. And as he fell asleep beside me, there were no words. No "I love you." No "Good night." Nothing, only silence. It took me a while to fall asleep. I kept hearing his words over and over again. I think it was close to dawn before I finally fell back to sleep.

When I woke up the next morning, I saw Drew lying on his side, facing me. I wondered how long he'd been staring at me. It made me feel a little uncomfortable. He didn't say anything. He still looked as grim as he had last night when he was telling me we weren't working.

"What time is it?

"Let's just say you won't make it to church on time."

He pushed the hair out of my face and ran his finger along my cheekbone. Still, he didn't make eye contact with me. I could still hear his words from last night in my head. Too many mixed signals were overloading my brain. I needed to know where I stood. I wasn't usually the aggressive one when it came to our physical relationship, but I proved I could be. I don't know what I thought it would do. I guess I wasn't enough to make him stay.

"Are you leaving me?"

He sat up and turned his back to me. My heart hurt as I sat next to him and put my hand on his forearm. I prayed under my breath.

"I don't want to hurt you, Grace," he turned to look at me,

but he only met my eyes briefly.

"And you don't think that leaving me is not going to hurt me?"

I said that, but it didn't sound like me. It was breathy and strained as I tried not to break down. Was last night all a physical response? Did it not mean anything to him? Did I not mean anything to him?

"Drew, I made a promise to you in front of God and a whole bunch of witnesses, and that still means something to me. I promised I'd be there for you when it got bad – you know the whole 'for better, for worse' part of the vows."

"And I promised to protect you."

"That wasn't in our vows."

"No, but it was in my heart. And so far, you've been part of three murder investigations in six months. That's insane. You've been kidnapped and threatened and - "

"And how could you have stopped that from happening?"

He shook his head.

"I don't know, but I look at you. You've lost weight; you don't smile; you don't laugh. You're not happy. Our marriage is crumbling around us, and I don't know how to fix it."

"Leaving is not going to fix it."

He shook his head.

"I don't want anything else to happen to you. It would be better if I weren't in your life."

"Stop it. I'm not listening to this anymore. You aren't going anywhere. My brother's birthday is today, and we are having lunch at my parents' house. Remember? So at least for today, stay."

"I'd forgotten about that."

"Zack was your best friend once. The two of you probably have more in common than you realize."

"I'll stay for today, but I can't make any more promises I can't keep."

"What's going on with you, Drew?"

"I just can't talk about it."

"Please."

He touched my cheek with his fingertips and shook his head. "I can't, Grace. Please understand."

I didn't think my heart could sink anymore, but it did.

"I don't understand."

He got out of bed and headed for the shower. I was tired of crying, but the tears flowed anyway.

I tried to put on a brave face at my parents' house. As soon as we arrived, I busied myself in the kitchen. My mother stared at me, but she didn't say much. I just shook my head when she tried. My sister-in-law helped put things on the table as my brother wrangled his kids in the other room.

Drew was quiet for most of the meal. There was small talk around the table, but I couldn't make eye contact with anyone. Thankfully, the topic of Bill's murder didn't come up. Of course, it wasn't polite dinner conversation. We talked about flowers and college football and nothing of importance. Zack talked about his new position; at least what he could tell us. My brother's kids ranged in age from 4 months through 7 years. The oldest two talked about school and the latest episode of whatever kids' show was popular. I wasn't really paying attention. Mama had made meatloaf because Zack always loved it. I didn't eat much of it. I wasn't hungry.

"Does anyone want cake?" Mama announced as the meal wound down.

"Me! Me!" the grandchildren shouted. The baby cried.

"I think that's my cue," my sister-in-law, Sarah, said as she carried the baby into the other room to nurse him.

"I'll help you, Mama."

I got up and went into the kitchen to help put the candles on the seven-layer cake - yes, it was seven layers of chocolate decadence.

"Are you okay?" she whispered.

"No, but I can't talk about it without crying. This is Zack's birthday, and I want it to be happy. Okay."

She nodded.

"I'm here for you, baby."

"I know."

She hugged me, and I brushed the tears away.

Right as my mother brought the cake out, Drew's phone began to ring. He jumped up and headed for the door.

I stole glances at my mother, Drew, my brother, and the door in a matter of seconds. He came back into the room to whisper in my ear.

"I might have a break in Bill's murder case. I'm sorry. I have to go," he said.

"I'll take Gracie home if Dad will let me borrow the car," Zack said. "You go and do your police work and let my baby sister have birthday cake."

Drew kissed me on the cheek and headed for the door. The kiss was for show. I knew that. I glanced at my brother who shot me a concerned look. After the cake and ice cream, which I just didn't feel like eating, there were presents. I wanted to enjoy this, but it was agonizing.

Zack let his children, his 7 year-old twin girls, Madison and Cason, and his 3 year-old son, Ben, open the gifts for him.

My mother always liked to get lots of small things, especially when she knew the kids were coming. There was nothing like watching kids tear into wrapping paper, even if it was covering pairs of socks and exciting things like that. She also included a couple of dolls for the girls. They thought that was hilarious that my mother would give dolls to their dad. But Ben thought it was great that Nana had given his daddy a toy car. Zack played it off perfectly and told them he wanted to give his presents away.

I envied him so much, especially now that my dreams of ever having children were slipping further away. I couldn't have children without a husband, and I didn't know how much longer I'd have one of those.

After the presents, Zack kissed Sarah and his kids and grabbed my dad's car keys. I gave Daddy a kiss on the cheek. He pulled me close for a moment.

"It's going to be okay, Gracie."

I wanted to cry. Of course, they could tell something was wrong. Everyone except the kids could.

I knew the minute we got into the car the questions would come. I braced for them.

"You're awfully quiet, sis."

"I'm an introvert, remember? I've had my people overload for the day."

He laughed.

"I think it's a little more than that."

When he pulled into my driveway, he turned to me.

"Mind if I walk you in?" he asked.

"Not at all."

It was still warm enough in October to sit outside. It was a beautiful night in Georgia.

I sat down on my front porch swing, and Zack joined me.

"You love Mama's seven-layer cake, and you didn't touch it."

"Not hungry, I guess."

"Liar. What's wrong?"

I shook my head.

"Nothing."

"You can't lie to your big brother. I want to know what's wrong with you and Drew."

I didn't know what to say. I bit my lip to try not to cry. I couldn't answer.

"Drew has been my friend for as long as I can remember. And he is not the same person I used to know. I mean, I've only seen him at Christmas the past few years, but he's so different."

The lip biting wasn't working, and the tears began to flow. I was too tired to stop them. I'd kept a straight face all night; I just couldn't anymore.

"When did he start acting different?"

I had to think about that for a minute, even though the names of Mark and Linda came immediately to my mind. He didn't act differently right away, though. It was subtle.

"Gracie, I think he's suffering from PTSD, and he needs help."

"PTSD?"

"Yes. I've been deployed three times, and I've seen it in my soldiers a lot. I know the signs, even the silent ones. He doesn't sleep, does he?"

I didn't know how to answer that. He slept but only after he'd been drinking.

"He's definitely not the fun-loving guy I once knew. And Mama told me about what happened last October. I think it started there."

I simply nodded while he talked.

"It's hard to see someone die. It's even harder when it's your friend, and you feel responsible."

"That's exactly how he feels."

"And she told me he almost lost you in April."

"She talks a lot, doesn't she?" I laughed weakly. "I left Drew, and then I got kidnapped. Dying crossed my mind a few times. Not that I wanted to die, but I thought it was a possibility. Yes, sir, April was a really fun month."

He nodded his head.

"And he's been drinking?"

"How did you know?"

"There's often a pattern to PTSD. It leads to substance abuse for a lot of people. I can get him some help."

Zack put his arm around me and pulled me in. I cried for a few minutes before pulling away and wiping the tears from my face.

"I had this dream the other night about him drowning and begging me to help him, and I felt powerless. I've tried, Zack. I really have tried."

"I know, Grace. He needs some help, and he needs to talk

to someone who knows about PTSD. Not everyone knows how to deal with it. Drew is a professional at hiding his emotions. He knows exactly what to say so no flags are raised. Mama said he went back to work quickly so he must've passed all the mental evaluations. I'm going to help you, Gracie, and I'm going to help him. I'm sorry I've been so busy with my career that I didn't reach out sooner."

"I don't blame you. You have a wife and four kids, and you're out saving the world with the Army every day."

"Yeah, yeah. But you're my kid sister, and I feel responsible in a way. That guy was my best friend, and I let him steal your heart. My own buddy stole my sister."

He laughed. I tried to laugh, too.

"You weren't here when he stole my heart."

"Liar. I remember how you looked at him even when you were 12."

I smiled.

"12? How about when I was 10?"

"I shouldn't have waited this long, Gracie. You're my first family, and big brothers are supposed to take care of their kid sisters."

He kissed me on the top of my head.

"Have you had PTSD?'

He nodded.

"Yeah. I've seen a lot of stuff, Gracie. Stuff I won't tell you about. Some things I can't tell you about - horrible things, things that I can't erase from my mind. And sometimes it's hard, especially when you see kids -" he paused and stared off into space. I wondered what he was reliving.

"But you have to process it and go on."

"Drew is so closed off to everyone."

"I think I can get through to him. I've seen some of the same things he has, and maybe I can rebuild that bridge between us. I know he went to see Pastor B, and faith definitely helped me through."

"He lost his faith a while back. We don't even talk about it anymore. He blames God for everything, I think. That used to be our common ground. We could always come back to that place, but now —"

"Faith is important to him, Grace. I know that, but sometimes, you have to combine your faith with some other steps. I can come at it from a different angle than you or Pastor B or most people he talks to. And I'm hoping he'll let his guard down with me. We may have a few years between us, but we have a lot in common. I think I can make him see that. And sometimes, it takes some medication to help."

"Yeah, like Drew is going to take meds for mental health."

"I know. Mental health still has a stigma, and especially in his line of work, it's going to be touchy. He's not going to want to lose his job or do anything to put it in jeopardy."

I took a deep breath.

"That's so true. You know I even think he feels threatened by me when it comes to his job. He keeps saying – 'my case, Grace, my investigation' like I really want to do his job."

"Listen, you worry about taking care of you, and I'll see what I can do for him."

"You don't think he'll be suspicious? I mean, you show up and then corner him on PTSD. He'll think I had something to do with it."

He laughed.

"He might be resistant at first, but he and I were blood brothers long before he married you. We made an oath and cut our wrists in the treehouse in the days when girls were still yucky."

I laughed. I could see the two of them doing something like that. They were best buddies at one time.

"And what about you? Three dead bodies in six months. You were the one who passed out at the sight of blood."

"I'm getting stronger. I guess."

"You should talk to someone, too."

"I was for a while, but –"

"But what?"

"He's been taking money out of our account and I couldn't afford a therapist anymore."

Zack didn't say anything for a moment.

"What's really going on, Grace?" he asked softly.

I couldn't answer. All the things I was holding inside came to the surface. He held me close and pushed the swing as I cried. When I finally could, I sat up and wiped away the tears.

"He told me that we weren't working and that he was leaving last night. He said he's talked to a lawyer."

"But, apparently, you convinced him to stay."

"For how long, I don't know. He's not here now; is he?"

The gentle rocking of the swing was soothing. I was glad to have someone besides Emmie to talk to. I didn't like telling her all my problems, and I tried not to burden my mother. I didn't want to turn her to be angry with Drew; I had enough anger and pain for everyone.

"Grace, it will all be okay. Somehow, some way. It's going to work out; you just have to believe that."

"I'll try, Zack. I really will."

"Do you want me to stay with you until he gets home?"

"No, I'm a big girl. I need some silence right now."

He nodded. He got me and my introverted qualities. He gave me a hug.

"Call me if you need anything."

I nodded.

"Please," he added.

"I will. Thank you."

He kissed the top of my head and went to the car. I watched as he drove away and then wandered into the house. I sat in the chair in our bedroom for a long time just thinking about life and wondering how I could breach the ever-increasing gap between my husband and me. I knew the anniversary was in just a few days. I'm sure that was the reason it had seemed to be worse over the past couple of weeks. But, in all honesty, it had steadily gone downhill since July. The few times we got together with Mark and Linda involved Independence Day celebrations. We had cookouts together. This year, we didn't do anything. We didn't even go see the fireworks. He stayed up much later than I did, and I wondered now if that's when he started drinking again.

About an hour after Zack left, Drew came home. I was still sitting in our bedroom in the dark staring off into space. He seemed surprised to see me when he turned on the light.

He pulled a duffle bag out of the closet and went to his dresser.

"I'm just going to get a few things and spend the night at Butch's house."

I nodded.

"Did you get a break in your case?"

"Yes, we did."

He was short.

"Any leads on Sunny Kim and the spa?"

"My investigation, Grace," he growled.

"I know. You know that Jimmy was at the spa yesterday."

I was babbling, trying to keep him at the house.

"My investigation, Grace," he glared at me. "And Sunny is in jail on separate charges after propositioning me when I went to interrogate her today."

"Oh."

I searched for something to say.

"You don't have to leave, Drew."

He stopped and turned to look at me, throwing a couple of pairs of socks into the bag.

"It's best for you that I go."

"Your rationale doesn't hold up."

"Damn it, Grace."

He slammed the drawer. He never cursed at me however mildly. I jumped.

"If I wasn't an officer of the law, you and Emmie wouldn't be staking out massage parlors or spying on people's parties or finding yourself kidnapped and almost killed. You need to have a life that doesn't include murder investigations and violence," he growled at me.

"But these murders I've seen had nothing to do with you. I was at the wrong place at the wrong time."

"But you are so bent on helping me solve these cases when I can do this on my own. I was trained to do this. If you were married to anyone else, you wouldn't be trying to solve crimes."

He took a deep breath.

"You're right, Drew."

"And since you can't stop yourself and let me do my job, I'm stopping it for you. Besides, I can't protect you from my own demons, Grace."

"And Butch is safe?"

"He doesn't question me about every little thing, and he doesn't pry into Mark and Linda's deaths. And that's where you are going with all of this, isn't it?"

"Did last night mean anything to you?"

He stared at me as though I'd hit him, then he shook his head.

"I will always love you, Grace. I just stopped being your knight in shining armor a long time ago."

I looked at the floor as he walked out of the bedroom. I heard the front door slam and his engine start. I sank to the floor and cried.

Of course, I didn't sleep much. I was restless, and finally around 3 a.m., I got up and decided to do some research. I was curious about what Zack had talked about – PTSD, short for post-traumatic stress disorder.

I found a few websites on the subject, and I could see Drew in their descriptions of the symptoms.

It wasn't limited to people in the military, although they did experience it and it was common for those involved in combat. Any traumatic experience could cause it. Sometimes, the symptoms show up early; at other times, it could take a while – months or even years.

Drew seemed to manage early on after the deaths of Mark and Linda. A couple of things seemed to jump off the page at me. He refused to talk about it and avoided all mention of it, and that was common. One website mentioned having negative feelings, and he had plenty of those. It mentioned guilt and shame. I'd often thought he blamed himself for their deaths and he felt he should've stopped them from happening.

The tears flowed even more as I read that people with PTSD had problems with substances, including drugs and alcohol, and they had relationship problems, including divorce. Zack knew what he was talking about. I knew the pending anniversary of that day was a trigger for some of the behavior, but the mood swings had been there for most of the summer and fall. He'd been drinking in the spring, but he'd stopped. He'd gone to some counseling, but it wasn't enough.

Other research told me what I already knew but showed me it wasn't my imagination that I was always walking on eggshells, wondering if anything I did or said would set him off, but the websites did tell me not to pressure him to talk. I guess I blew that one. The more I read, the more I realized I hadn't acted like the research said I should. Now, I felt guilty that I'd responded in the wrong way. Maybe some of this was my fault. Like I needed more things to make me feel guilty.

8

Because of Dana's health and the autopsy, Bill's funeral had been delayed a couple of days. I wasn't sure who was helping plan it.

I was in much earlier than usual on Monday. It was hard to believe that Bill was killed a few days before. It seemed like months. It was a good thing I got there early because there were things left over from the weekend. I kept some makeup at work, which was another good thing. I tried to make myself somewhat presentable just in case a customer or two came in. I didn't need to scare them away. With the bags and dark circles under my eyes, I just needed a black cape and a black wig to complete my vampire look. Oh well, Halloween was around the corner. I supposed I could play it off. Fortunately, the concealer I used did wonders. I fended off the Dracula's Bride look for now.

Beth was still out of town; Jazzy had school; and Emmie had some loose ends to tie up with her FBI job, so it was all going to be on me, not that I minded. There was too much going on in my head, and I really didn't want to talk to Emmie about it. I wasn't sure if my husband would be at home when I got there despite the time we'd spent together a few nights before. He seemed insistent that we were done. And Saturday was just one single night in more than a decade of nights. I guess it couldn't make up for all the underlying turmoil.

I'd only been open about 30 minutes when I heard the bell ring. I'd been in the work area and walked into the retail part of the shop. I glanced at the customer entering, and I was thankful that I wasn't holding anything, or I probably would've dropped it.

I'd always said that I loved Drew my whole life, and that was partially true. My crush on him developed when I was a kid, but there was a time in my life when that relationship seemed somewhere between highly unlikely and downright impossible. He was older; he wasn't a part of my life after Zack joined the Army, and it wasn't until I was in college that he even knew I existed as someone besides his best friend's little sister. I didn't date a lot of people before Drew, but there was one person who I had imagined spending my life with before Drew came back into the picture. His name was Trevor Blake. He wasn't the star of the football team; he ran cross country. He had beautiful unruly, curly blonde hair, piercing blue eyes, and the most beautiful tenor voice. He and I sang in the high school chorus together. The alto section was next to the tenors, and Trevor and I met while singing in third period at the beginning of his senior year of high school. He was two years older than me, and we dated for about two years. He stayed in Augusta for his first year of college, but his parents thought he needed to leave the area - and me - so they pressured him into applying to the University of Georgia, where everyone else in his family had graduated from. He transferred after that first year and headed to Athens. I was heartbroken. He said we'd stay in touch, but I knew better. I knew it meant goodbye, and the final goodbye came during the Christmas holidays, when he told me his parents wanted him to focus on school and not on a relationship. He was simply too young, they said. My heart was crushed. After I reconnected with Drew, I convinced myself that Drew had been my one and only love, and that what I'd experienced with Trevor was only an infatuation. But part of me knew better. Trevor was different from Drew.

I hadn't seen him since that day when he dropped me off after a breakup date with my heart shattered, but there he was standing in my flower shop. I knew he was in town because Emmie said she saw him at Bill's party, but I didn't see him then. I couldn't breathe as I saw him come in with his big smile.

"Grace," he said my name as he walked toward me and gave me a huge bear hug. I was stunned and at the same time, I felt a flutter. No, I couldn't feel any fluttering. Maybe that was just the pieces of my broken heart remembering the first time they'd been shattered. I wasn't sure what this emotional response was, but it made me feel extremely uncomfortable. Things could've been very different if he and I hadn't been so young. I tried not to prolong the hug. I moved back behind my counter to put distance between us.

"Trevor, what a surprise. I thought you lived in Charlotte."

Those words tumbled out of my mouth. I couldn't think of anything intelligent to say.

"I did, but I'm back for a while."

I smiled, and he nodded. I stared at him. He hadn't changed at all. He still had the tousled blonde curls and those deep blue eyes. For a split second, I wished he was 18 and I was 16 again. I could erase all the pain I'd felt over the past year. I wondered if I'd covered up all the dark circles, and what my hair looked like. Was I a mess? This conversation was awkward, and I wasn't sure what to say to him, so I changed the subject.

"What can I help you with?"

He smiled.

"Well, I have a couple of flower-related requests."

"Then you've come to the right place."

I tried to smile. I tried to slip into professional mode. I put my hands on the counter to keep them from shaking.

"You were always creative, Grace. I remember some of the things you came up with for the scenery for the spring musical."

I smiled. I was in charge of props that year, and they needed some flower arrangements for a wedding scene. It was one of my first attempts at arranging flowers. One of the cast member's mother was a florist. She provided some of the materials and gave me some hints. Of course, it turned into a disaster when one of the actors knocked over a column with a gorgeous floral arrangement I'd made. At least, no one got hurt or died like they seemed to be doing whenever I was around these day. Maybe I've always been bad luck when it came to flowers. I seemed to spell doom wherever I put my hand.

He started to laugh and so did I. It wasn't funny at the time. It was a nightmare. Trevor tried to save the flower arrangement from crashing to the floor, but as he did, he fell into another actor who bumped into someone else, and there was a heap of people on the floor. It was a comedy of errors. But they stayed in character and finished the scene. I had to hand that to them.

"You stayed in character. I think you even managed to sing while the disaster happened."

He gave a mock bow.

"Yes, I did," he smiled at me.

"Well, despite the disaster, I managed to make a career of this."

"That wasn't your fault. Your flowers weren't to blame. If I'm remembering them correctly, they were stunning. That's why I tried to save them."

"I don't know about that. Those were my first efforts. Anyway, it seems like disaster follows wherever I'm doing flowers these days."

He raised an eyebrow and tilted his head to the side.

"There have been three murders near where I've done flowers in the past six months. I'm feeling like I'm cursed or something."

"It's not your fault Bill was killed – unless you did it of course."

"No. I didn't like the man, but I didn't want him dead."

"I saw you Friday night. That's the reason I'm here."

I glanced away.

"I didn't see you."

"That's because my cousin has been cruel to you on more than one occasion, and you hid in the corner all night in hopes he wouldn't see you. But he did and almost made a scene."

I looked away. He was watching me just as Emmie had said. How had I not seen him?

"No need to be embarrassed. I could see you were well-protected, which is the reason I stayed away at the party."

I smiled. "I'm sorry for your loss."

"Don't be."

I must've reacted to that.

"Let's just say that Bill and I didn't exactly get along. He was like the brother I never wanted."

He gave me a weak smile. He didn't elaborate, and I wasn't going to ask.

"I'm sorry."

He brushed past that comment.

"Grace, I need to apologize to you for all those years ago."

"Trevor, all those years ago is right. You don't have to say anything."

He looked down at the counter.

"It wasn't my mother."

I nodded. Trevor was born when his mother was in her early 40s. His father was a doctor and a decade older than his mother. They already had three children when Trevor came along. Trevor's father wanted Trevor to become a doctor just like his three older brothers and himself. His father had passed away a couple of years ago. I knew because I made a lot of arrangements for him. I sent one of my own. I got a card from his mother, but Trevor didn't show up in my shop then. I wondered why he was here now.

"I was sorry to hear about your dad."

He nodded without answering. He seemed to ignore that remark completely.

"After all these years, I still really hate how our relationship ended. Maybe we were young, but … I didn't want to hurt you."

"It's in the past. It's fine. You said you wanted flowers."

I couldn't read his expression. He seemed like he was searching for something else to say so I got the conversation back on track for him.

"Yes, I need a funeral arrangement for Bill."

"Were you just in town for the party and now the funeral?"

"No, I'm going to be here for a while, I'm afraid. Mama was diagnosed with breast cancer a couple of months ago. Things don't look good. She's going through some radiation treatments, but – "

He paused and took a deep breath.

"I'm going to take care of her and try to make up for lost time. My brothers are too busy with their practices. They have home health nurses and are making sure my mother is medically stable, but I want to provide her emotional support. My sisters-in-law are great, but they have their lives, too, and they have kids who are all at the age where my sisters-in-law spend a lot of time driving. Since I'm not married, I can focus all my attention on my mother."

"That's so sweet, Trevor. I remember your mother as a special lady. She always made me feel welcomed."

I had always felt nervous around his father, but his mother always made me feel at ease. We even spent time together without Trevor.

He smiled.

"Mama always said not to send flowers to her funeral. She believes flowers are for the living so while she's still alive I'm going to make sure she has plenty of them. She loves lilies, mainly stargazer lilies and calla lilies, and I want beautiful ones for her. I'd like you to make some arrangements for her - at least one a week, maybe more as time gets closer."

He paused and smiled weakly. I smiled.

"I can tell you have a lot of things you'd like to ask, but that Southern sensibility of not prying is standing in the way."

I laughed. I could hear my mother telling me not to ask too many questions, especially personal ones.

"Well, I haven't seen you in 15 years. To be honest, I'm surprised to see you. I'm not really sure what to say."

I was blurting out all kinds of stuff today. I could kick myself. I felt so stupid. Why was he having this effect on me?

"Yes, I followed my father's dream, and I became an

oncologist. I'm taking a leave of absence from the practice I'm in, but to be honest, I'm not sure if I'm going back to Charlotte. And as I said, I'm not married, and I'm not seeing anyone at the moment."

He looked directly at me when he said that, but it didn't matter because I was very married - or at least I thought I was. I was still an emotional mess. I needed to steer this conversation somewhere else.

"When is the funeral?"

"Wednesday. Dana's supposed to be on bedrest, but she's going to try to go to the funeral. Her mother is staying with her. My brothers and I helped make the arrangements for her yesterday."

"I saw her a couple of days ago. You could've just called me; you didn't have to come in."

"I wanted to see you in person – to talk to you. It's good to see you, Grace. You're still as beautiful as ever."

I wasn't expecting that. His voice was soft, and I think I blushed when he said that. I haven't blushed in years. I glanced away. Well, earlier I had thought of the possibility of being 16 again, and it was here. I was acting just like a lovestruck puppy.

"Thank you."

"We're out a lot so I don't want the flowers delivered. I'll pick them up. My mother has appointments for her radiation and then there are other doctors we see. The list is endless. I'd like to get the first one today."

"I can have something ready after lunch. Is that soon enough?"

He nodded and headed to the door. My hands were shaking at my side, and I felt my knees buckling. Why now? Why today? And why was he telling me his whole life story? My life seemed to be falling apart around me. I still had Drew's words about us not working ringing in my ears, and I wasn't strong enough to deal with everything I was already going through much less seeing the man who probably was my first love. If I ever wanted to run away and hide, it was now. Usually, I liked being alone, but this was one time I really wished someone else was here with me.

"Focus, Grace. You've got to focus," I said out loud.

I went to the office and pulled the orders for the morning. I hadn't had so many orders in a long time. There were several for Bill's funeral and some for new babies. How was I going to get this all done by myself? I felt like crying. I was overwhelmed, but I was grateful to have the work. I could focus my attention somewhere besides my personal life. I just had to get everything finished and then I could make the deliveries myself. I had come in at 8:30 and Trevor was my first and only customer who walked through the door. As I concentrated on making the arrangements, time seemed to fly by. I finished three small baby arrangements before I tackled the larger funeral sprays. Maybe Jazzy could make these deliveries for me after she got finished with her classes.

I had managed to put men out of my mind for a couple of hours at least.

I was putting some final touches on one of the funeral sprays when I heard the bell ring. I walked out of the work room and saw Trevor had returned. I looked at the clock. It was nearly 2 p.m.

"How can it be so late?"

I was frazzled. I glanced at him, and I glanced at the clock again.

"What's wrong?" he asked.

"I'm so sorry. So sorry. I haven't finished your arrangement. The time slipped away from me. I can have it done if you want to come back or you can wait."

He smiled. "Grace, it's okay. I'm not in a hurry."

"I'm so sorry. I didn't mean for you to waste a trip."

"The trip wasn't wasted. I can come back."

He paused for a minute.

"I take it that means you haven't had lunch, either."

"Lunch?" I shook my head. I hadn't even taken a bathroom break. "I don't even know what that is on some days."

"I'll be back. Take your time. There's a nurse with Mama right now, and Mama is probably taking her afternoon nap anyway. She sleeps a lot these days."

I nodded.

"Give me 30 minutes, and I promise I'll have something for you."

"Grace, it's okay," he said.

I rushed into the stock room and pulled all the lilies I could find. I loved the colors in stargazer lilies and their rich pinks paired well with red and white roses and carnations. The arrangement almost looked like something for Valentine's Day or Christmas rather than fall with all those rich colors, but it was beautiful. I hoped he didn't think it looked too romantic for his mother. I guess I knew where my subconscious was because romance was not what my brain was going for.

When Trevor returned, I was finished with the arrangement, and I realized I was starving.

He was carrying a bag. He set it on the counter and pulled out two round aluminum foil containers and a white bag with spots of oil bleeding through. I knew exactly what that was – Mexican food - and it smelled wonderful.

"Two cheese enchiladas with rice and guacamole."

"Thank you. How much do I owe you?"

"This is on me."

"You don't have to."

"I think it was one of the lunch specials today, so it's not a big deal," he said. "I was really looking forward to Teresa's. Teresa's is now a meat market, and the Chinese restaurant is now a Mexican one. I'm so confused."

I laughed.

"It has been a while since you've been here."

Teresa's was our favorite date location, and I ate the same thing every time we went out. I was predictable, and the fact that he remembered what I ate was making me more uncomfortable by the minute. I checked my phone. There wasn't a single text from Drew and no missed calls. I wasn't good with small talk, and I still wasn't sure what to make of Trevor having lunch with me.

"How long have you been in town?"

"About three weeks. I had to settle patients and get some things squared away before I could move down here. It's been strange coming back to Augusta. You know that saying about you can never go home. You can't really. Everything is different, and I didn't realize I had so many demons to face here. You don't get that when you are only in town a few days at a time."

"What are they saying about your mother?"

"It's all pretty iffy right now. She's a fighter. She might make it through the holidays or she might not. She's had several other illnesses in the past few years that could compound the effect the cancer has. This whole thing with Bill has really upset her. It hasn't been good."

I listened while searching for something to say to fill the awkward gaps. We talked about people we went to school with, hitting the highlights of the marriages, divorces, and births of their children.

"Thank you for lunch."

"My pleasure, and it's not a problem. How've you been, Grace?"

A poker face was something I did not have. I couldn't hide my emotions at all, and I'm glad I didn't have a mirror. I didn't think this would be pretty. I tried to smile, but I was wondering how well Trevor still knew me. I didn't answer right away, so in a way, I guess I did answer. My delay wasn't lost on him.

"That good, huh?"

"It's been a tough year. I think I told you earlier that my flowers had been at the scene where three different murders had taken place this year."

"You did."

"I still see their faces. I found them all. Sometimes I don't sleep at night. Death and suffering end up in my dreams."

Maybe I didn't have to delve into any personal details. Three murders were enough to ruin anyone's year, weren't they?

"Ah, your dreams."

He knew about my dreams. They prepared me for him breaking up with me. I'd had several dreams after he left for Georgia. Of course, I passed it off to my angst and me worrying that it was going to happen. And there were a couple of other odd dreams that happened while he and I dated. I dreamed about one of the people in his class dying in a car accident, and two weeks later, she'd wrapped her 16th birthday present around a tree.

"Do you have them a lot?"

I nodded.

"Have you talked to anyone about your stress?"

I stared at him. He sounded just like my brother.

"I thought you were an oncologist not a psychiatrist."

He laughed.

"Mental and physical health often go hand in hand."

"I've gone some, but I've been so busy lately I haven't been able to break away."

That was a small lie. I wasn't good at lying, but I didn't want to tell him the real reason I hadn't gone back.

"I talk to Emmie, and I still pray. And there's healing in my flowers. Something about the way they smell and the way they feel, and when I give them to people and get to see them smile. I don't know. It brings comfort to me."

"Emmie, your partner in crime. How is she?"

"She's great. Single mom of two boys. She's been working for the FBI as a sketch artist, or a forensic artist, I think is her title. I'm trying to convince her to have an art show – not of dead bodies though."

He laughed and glanced around.

"You could probably have a small exhibit here with a reception. That would be great.

Has your husband found any clues about my cousin's killer?"

He made no transition between those two thoughts. I wondered if he'd just been waiting to ask me about it, but then he didn't give me time to answer.

"My mother is very upset by all of this. She wants to go to Bill's funeral, but I don't know if that's a good idea."

"I know he has leads, but that's all I know. They obviously haven't arrested anyone."

I didn't look at him when I said that. I didn't know how to say it without it coming across like I didn't talk to my husband. He didn't need to know Drew and I were having problems.

"What kinds of leads?" he paused. "If I might ask, that is."

"Well I think anyone at the party was a suspect since he was killed there. Drew's been working late, so I'm sure he's onto something."

"Mama asks a lot of questions because no one is offering her any information. She keeps calling Dana. I'm not sure it's good for Dana, if you know what I mean."

I didn't know if I should share everything I knew; not that I knew much.

"I saw Dana the other day. She's a wreck."

"Indeed, and asking her too many questions isn't good. I'm sorry if this puts you in an uncomfortable situation. I guess conversations between a deputy and his wife are as privileged as those between a doctor and patient."

"I don't know much. I think we know Bill had some enemies out there. I'm still not sure how he actually thought he would be elected mayor."

"I was thinking the same thing."

There was an awkward pause, and I ate quickly. I had to finish a few more things. Jazzy was scheduled to come in within 30 minutes to make deliveries for me.

"I finished the arrangement. Let me get it for you."

I went into the back and brought it out.

"That's beautiful. She will love it," he said.

He handed me his credit card.

"Are you sure?"

"It has lilies and roses. It's sure to make her happy. You remember she was a master gardener."

I smiled. Mrs. Blake had the most beautiful rose garden at one time.

"I'll deliver the funeral spray to the funeral home this afternoon."

"Thank you. Are you planning on going to the funeral?"

"No. I'll go to the funeral home to see Dana tomorrow night, but I'll be here Wednesday."

As I handed the card back to him, our hands briefly touched. What was wrong with me? I had to keep reminding myself I was a married woman. I could see that ring when I looked at my hand. Why did I find him so attractive still?

"I'll see you soon, Grace."

He took a business card out of his wallet. He picked up a pen from the counter, and I watched as he wrote something down on the card. He handed it to me. I hesitated at taking it.

"In case you have any information on the case you could share with me."

Reluctantly, I took it. He'd written his personal cell number on it.

"If Drew shares anything, I'll let you know."

I swallowed as I watched him leave. I had to shake this. I should be angry. He broke my heart all those years ago, and he was waltzing back into my life now, telling me he's single and available. And I couldn't figure out why he would do this now after all these years. I went into the bathroom and stared at myself in the mirror. I guess I didn't look too frazzled. I splashed some cold water on my face. I closed the door and took a few deep breaths. I could get through anything, and this was nothing I couldn't handle. Or at least that's what I told myself.

Jazzy arrived in time to make some of my deliveries while I

finished the final orders for the day. When she got back, she could make another run.

It was strange not to at least get a text from Drew. I replayed parts of the weekend, especially when he told me he was going to leave. It was like a knife in my heart every time I thought of it. It was almost time to close the shop when I called him, but he didn't answer. I guess I should've expected that. I didn't want to go home so I called the next best thing.

"Could I come to your house tonight, Emmie?"

"The boys are at soccer practice with their dad. He's their coach, and he's supposed to bring them home. I'll see if he'll switch nights with me. Is this a Three Stooges kind of night or do I need to break out the tissues and chick flicks?"

"I'm tired of crying, Emmie. I need something incredibly stupid and funny at the same time."

"I think I have just the thing."

As I began to head out, I noticed Trevor's card on the counter. I picked it up and stared at it. I took it into my office and put it in my desk drawer.

Emmie was ready when I got there. She opened the door before I could.

"You look horrible, Grace."

"Thanks, Emmie. I appreciate it. I feel horrible."

"I have chocolate chip cookie dough ice cream plus extra chocolate chips."

"I'm not hungry, Emmie. I just didn't want to go home."

She put her hands on her hips and stared at me.

"This is serious."

"Drew left me. He's called an attorney, and I don't want to talk about this anymore."

Emmie's mouth dropped, and I fell into her couch. She had one of those couches that wrapped its cushions around you and didn't let you get up. I could put my feet on her furniture without hearing my mom's voice in my head telling me to put my feet down. I pulled my feet under me on the couch and grabbed a couple of pillows, hugging them to me. I'd held the tears in all day. I couldn't anymore.

"You can't just make that announcement, hon, and not say anything else."

"I don't want to talk about it. You know everything that's gone on. He said we weren't working."

"I can't believe it. He loves you."

"The ironic thing is he said that's the reason he left me because he loves me."

"No wonder you look as awful as you do."

"Thanks. Just what I wanted to hear especially when Trevor Blake showed up in my shop. I haven't seen him in ages. Not the impression I wanted to give."

"Trevor?"

I nodded.

"You need to run as fast as you can from that situation."

"What situation? He wants flowers for Bill's funeral and arrangements for his mother who has cancer."

"Did he give you his number?"

I stared at her. I wasn't sure where she was headed.

"You're very vulnerable right now, Grace. Your husband just left. You've seen three murders, lost another baby and been kidnapped in the past year."

"Yes, I remember all of that very well. I didn't need to be reminded."

"My point is your emotions are not stable, and the last thing you need is someone complicating matters for you. From the sounds of it, he's vulnerable, too. You could both get very hurt in all of this."

"Oh, I think matters have gone beyond complicated. You know what? Coming to see you was a bad idea. I don't need you lecturing me. I still have morals. I'm not going to cheat on my husband – for however much longer he is my husband. Trevor came into my shop. He ordered flowers. He asked me about the investigation because he's related to Bill, and you yourself told me he was there Friday night. I'm sorry you arranged for the kids not to be here."

With every word, my voice got louder. I broke free of the couch, stood up, and grabbed my shoes.

"Sit down, Grace Ward."

I stared at Emmie. That was the tone she used with her boys. I pointed at her.

"If one more person treats me like I'm a preschooler, I will hurt them."

I made sure to enunciate all those words.

"Please, Grace."

"Then leave this alone. I'm not running off to sleep with Trevor, okay? You of all people should know me better than that. That's the last thing I want to do."

She nodded.

"I'm sorry, Grace. But hurting people do crazy things sometimes, and the two of you have a history. I just don't want to see you hurting."

"I'm very aware of that history. Who knows what might've happened there, but it didn't. I can't go back and change anything. And what else could possibly make me hurt any more than I already am?"

"Grace, you know you're the sister I never had, and I will always love you and I will always be concerned about you. Besides, Trevor is hot, and we both know it."

Only Emmie would throw a comment in like that. And her goal of getting me to laugh worked. I did, if only for a minute.

"Look, Emmie. I will admit Trevor is more handsome now than he was in high school, but I'm not going to do anything. I promised never to cheat on Drew, and he hasn't even been gone 24 hours yet. Do you want me to set the two of you up on a date? He asked about you."

She paused for a moment.

"I could think of worse people to go out with than Trevor

Blake."

"I'm not interested, Emmie. Drew may come home even though he's not answering his phone or my texts. What I am interested in is not feeling like I have a hole where my heart is supposed to be."

She gave me a hug.

"I know, just don't try to fill that hole right now, okay?"

When she let go of me, I saw a glimmer of mischief in her eyes. She had a certain smile I knew too well. It meant she had a juicy secret she couldn't wait to tell.

"What, Emmie?"

"Well, I have some info on Bill's murder if you're interested." She grinned.

I just stared at her.

"Don't raise your eyebrow at me like that, Grace Ward," she said. "You know you want to know."

I sat back down on her couch and got comfortable.

"I'm all ears."

I tried to be enthusiastic about it, but I think my words fell flat.

"I have a couple of sources who tell me that ballistics –"

I interrupted.

"Who is your source?"

She grinned and raised an eyebrow.

"I have to protect them."

"Oh really?"

"Of course. It's Butch. He still wants to go out with me."

"Okay."

"So, it looks like an antique gun killed Bill. And someone tried to pawn this really old gun over the weekend. They claimed to have found it. The pawn shop owner thought it was suspicious and called it in. This gun looks to have been specially made. It has a mother of pearl inlay. Very small. Like it was made for a woman and maybe early 20th century. But it's not registered. They think it might have been a collector's piece, probably kept in a family."

I nodded.

"That's not uncommon."

"No, but it narrows it down."

"Maybe. I don't know if I care."

"Could it belong to Jimmy Hughes?" she asked.

"You think?"

"It's possible. He has an extensive gun collection."

"I think that could be said about a lot of people who were at the party."

"Oh, and about Ray Finch. Apparently, he was supposed to be Bill's image man."

"Image man? I thought he was the campaign manager."

"Yes, he was supposed to paint Bill as the doting family man concerned with the needs of Augustans."

"Uh-huh."

"You sound skeptical, sweetie."

"How you could even say that with a straight face is beyond me, Emmie!"

She smiled and then burst out laughing.

"You're right. But should we be saying bad things about Bill since he's dead?"

"So, Ray Finch was supposed to come in and clean up Bill's image."

"Yes, my FBI friends said Ray is clean. He doesn't have any kind of a record. He pays his taxes, never cheated on his wife that we can find, goes to church every Sunday, volunteers at the children's hospital. And he has an alibi for Friday night around the time of the murder. He was having dinner with his wife; they have a credit card receipt from almost the exact time of the murder. The manager of the restaurant verified both of them were there."

"We need Beth. She'd give us the low down on him. She'll know."

Emmie started scrolling through her phone. "I'm one step

ahead of you. Beth sent me a text – 'Don't believe everything you read.'"

"Hmm. Well, you know what they say – birds of a feather.'"

"Sounds like it. I guess Bill was hoping Ray's exterior squeaky-clean appearance would rub off on him."

"Is that all?"

"No, Ray was brokering some kind of deal to get the massage parlor out of Bill's name and under a company called Paragon Investments."

"Okay. Paragon. Like a paragon of virtue? Bill wasn't that."

"No, he wasn't."

"Wait a second. You talked to Butch, and he didn't tell you that Drew spent the night on his couch?"

She bit her lip.

"You knew this whole time and didn't say anything?"

"Guilty."

"Drew didn't say anything about me?"

"Not that Butch told me. Butch just said that Drew needed some space and asked if he could crash with him a couple of days."

I nodded. That hurt.

"Okay Grace. Now, it's time for the good stuff. I Love Lucy episodes. Or what about Carol Burnett?"

"Harvey Korman and Tim Conway?"

She nodded. I'm not sure if I even focused on them although I loved how Tim Conway could keep a straight face while Harvey Korman couldn't stop laughing. Comedy geniuses, all of them. But tonight, not even Tim Conway's little old man could make me laugh.

Emmie grabbed my hand and squeezed it as I checked my phone for what must've been the hundredth time.

"It's going to be okay."

The next morning, Emmie headed to the FBI and I headed to my shop. More orders for Bill's funeral. I knew I needed to at least stop by the funeral home to see Dana.

9

There were more orders for Bill's funeral than I would've thought. Jazzy didn't have as many classes on Tuesdays, and I was so glad she could come in.

"From the way you talked about this man, I didn't think he'd have this many friends to come to a funeral," she said.

"You aren't kidding, Jazzy, but as I've always said, I think people really loved Dana. She was a saint to put up with him as long as she did. The flowers aren't for the dead; they are for the living. They are for the families left behind."

"Have you heard from Drew?"

I hadn't told her about Drew, but I guess good news traveled fast around here. I only shook my head. I kept reading the newspaper to see if there were any breaks in the case, but no arrests had been made. The longer it took to break a case, the more stressed Drew got. I'd thought about texting him, but I figured he'd only take that as a sign I was trying to get information from him, so I didn't. And he wasn't texting me.

At least, the funeral would keep me busy for one more day. To paraphrase a famous Southern belle - I could worry about things tomorrow. I didn't have to today.

Around noon, Jimmy Hughes came in.

"How's my little lady?"

I managed a weak smile as he gave me a kiss on the cheek. I

tried not to show my disgust for him.

"I've been hearing things I don't want to hear, little lady."

"Good news travels around Augusta faster than one of those Japanese bullet trains."

"Drew's a fool. I'm beginning to think all of them are. Bill cheating on Dana. Drew leaving you. What's wrong with them?"

He sounded angry. I'd never heard Jimmy angry. I shrugged my shoulders.

"Your husband paid me a visit, and he didn't look all too happy when he came to my house to talk to me. He went through my gun collection and was asking me all sorts of questions."

"I guess you gave him good answers because you are still on this side of a jail cell."

"He was looking for something really specific when he asked about the gun. He tried to throw in other questions to get me off-kilter, but there was something specific he was going for."

"Oh?"

"Yep. But I couldn't help him. I didn't know anything about the gun. Now if he'd asked me more about Bill, I could've helped him."

I nodded. He scowled as he put his hands on his hips.

"You seem a little different today, and it's not because of Drew."

"Why did Bill have photos of you and a half-dressed, barely more than a teenage girl? She better have been more than a teenager."

His mouth dropped, and he dropped his head.

"You know about them too?"

"Yes, I saw them. Why did Bill have them?"

"I already told Drew those aren't what they look like."

"That's what they all say."

I folded my arms against my chest.

"I promise you it's not."

"Jimmy, it's pretty damning."

"Yes, and if Peggy saw them, my head would be on a platter. There wouldn't be enough flowers in all of Georgia and South

Carolina combined to get me out of that doghouse. That was Bill's doing. He sent a stripper to me on my birthday. I didn't know what was happening. When those clothes started coming off, I started yelling. You don't see that in those photos. It's not what you think. The rest of the story is I stopped her before she finished and yelled at him to get out of my shop."

"It still looks pretty incriminating. Especially when it looks like she's sitting in your lap."

"I know. I didn't realize he kept those. He promised me he'd destroy them. He said it was all a joke."

Jimmy's face fell.

"I love Peggy. I wouldn't do anything to hurt her. You have to believe me. Bill said it was just a practical joke. She didn't even look like she was old enough to be doing that."

"I'll agree with you on that one."

"Did you know he left Dana practically penniless? He took my money and bought a business, which your husband has shut down, by the way. I confronted Bill a couple of days ago about it. He made me so mad. I could've – "

He paused. His face had started to turn red. He took a deep breath.

"Killed him? Someone did that, Jimmy. And my hus -. And Drew is trying to figure out who it was."

"And he was going to run for mayor. Had he lost his ever-loving mind? Who would've voted for that man?"

"Not me."

"He was such a snake. This town is better off without him. And so is Dana. I'd like to pat however did this on the back."

I had no idea Jimmy felt so strongly about anything.

"Obviously, he was able to charm some people."

"Yes, he swindled a lot of people, especially the ones who cared about him. He took money from Harper Blake, and that woman is dying. Plus, I think he took some from one of her sons."

"Trevor?"

"Oh, not Trevor. Trevor and Bill had a lot of bad blood. Trevor always saw through him and didn't have any time for Bill. But Harper always had a soft spot for Bill. She's a kind woman, and Trevor resented Bill for the way he manipulated to get Harper's attention. Trevor, though, he's the apple of Harper's eye. I don't know why he would've even been jealous of Bill."

"Trevor didn't talk about Bill when I knew him. I think Bill had already gone away to school by that time."

I shook my head. I just didn't get any of this. I stared at Jimmy. Could he possibly have killed Bill? Was he implying that Trevor might've? I wasn't sure, but there were things that just didn't add up. And why did everyone tell me their secrets, knowing what my husband did for a living?

"How did people get away with it, Jimmy? I mean, Bill scheming them."

"He made good on a lot of promises to me. I didn't know everything he was involved in until recently. He had me snowed. And now I'm so angry with being used by him."

Jimmy shook his head. I wanted to know more about Bill and the Blakes so I reopened that train of thought.

"So, Bill was close to the Blakes?"

"Not all of them. Harper always loved him. She has such a good heart, and none of her boys could do wrong in her sight – not one, even the one she adopted so to speak. And out of the goodness of her heart, she would give him anything he asked. She wouldn't have thought it was being swindled at all. Those boys would do just about anything to protect her," he said.

"How do you know Bill took money from her?"

"Well, he didn't steal it. He probably just sweet-talked her out of it. And when Trevor found out, he wasn't happy."

"I don't really know any of the Blakes except Trevor and I knew his mother. His dad didn't like me from what I remember. Even though it's been a long time, Trevor doesn't seem like the murdering kind."

"You dated Trevor, didn't you? You're right though, I can't see Trevor harming anyone."

"Yes, that was a long time ago," I paused. "Was there anyone in this town that Bill didn't swindle?"

"Sugar, I think you're probably the only one."

"Well, I had nothing to give him, and he hated me."

"Hate's a strong word, little lady, but he was always afraid of Drew, probably because he knew Drew was watching him."

"Really? How did I not know my own husband was watching Bill?"

"He didn't tell you everything, sweetheart, and you know it."

He had that correct. I wondered how much I even knew Drew.

"Do you have any idea who might've done this, Jimmy? You're still at the top of my suspect list."

"I made a list for your husband, but I could make you one, too."

He winked at me.

"All joking aside, it could've been anyone in that room."

"I heard he had a blowout with Ray Finch."

"Yup, I heard that, too. Ray didn't like the way Bill treated women."

"Then why was he Bill's campaign manager?"

"I'd heard he was trying to reform Bill in some way. He tried to get him to go to some counseling."

"I heard he was only there to clean up Bill's image."

"What a better way to clean up someone's image than to actually clean them up?"

"Then what was the argument about?"

"Bill was overhead making some comments about Sunny Kim, and I won't talk that way in front of a lady. But from the sounds of the conversation, he and Sunny were more than business partners - if you know what I mean."

"Yes, I think I do."

"Bill said he was trying to make an honest woman out of Sunny Kim by giving her a job, but she had ideas that – well I can't talk about them in the company of ladies."

"Oh shug, it's nothing I've never heard before," said Jazzy, who had been listening in the background.

I smiled.

"I went to confront Sunny about it the day after he was killed. She didn't deny it. She said she was just using him and his money to get ahead. But really, she was using my money. I hate all of it."

I took a deep breath and didn't answer. Jimmy's cell phone rang.

"One second, hon," he said.

He fumbled in his pocket, and I noticed he had not one, but two cell phones. Jimmy's personal and work cell phone had always been the same. I thought it was odd that he'd have another one now after all this time.

"I'll have to call you back" was the only thing he said, but the caller seemed to have agitated him. He smiled and looked at me.

"The reason for my visit. I want to do the nice thing and send an arrangement – for Dana, of course. It's not out of respect for Bill because I have none for him."

Any talk of the murder investigation was over. I guess asking about the insurance policy was not possible now. He wanted an arrangement for Dana. I knew that one. As the day progressed, I knew I'd have to pay my respects to her also. I'd been so preoccupied I had only been able to send a couple of short texts to her to let her know I was thinking of her and would come by as soon as I could break away.

Bill's funeral kept me busy most of the day, but I did swing by the funeral home during the visitation that night. I went hoping to see Dana, but she wasn't there. There were a lot of people there. It was so crowded, but I expected that. I saw Trevor and immediately recognized his brothers. They were the reasons for all the flowers. No one really cared about Bill, but the Blakes were well-respected. And as

Trevor had said, Bill was the brother he never asked for, adopted into Trevor's family.

I slipped into the building among the throng of people and found my way to the guest book. I was so used to writing "Drew and Grace Ward" on the line, but this time, I stood there with the pen in my hand. I swallowed and simply wrote my own name. This was starting to sink in. I hadn't heard anything from Drew in two days. Throughout our marriage, we talked or texted every day. It was rare, but he and I had only been separated for a few days for conferences or other business-related things our entire marriage. Even then, the day never ended without some type of communication between us.

I put the pen down and wiped away a couple of tears. I was holding up the line, and I knew it. I headed straight toward the back door without looking around at anyone. I was finding it hard to breathe, and I needed to get away from people who might ask me questions.

The door closed behind me, but I heard it open again.

"Who knew Bill had so many friends?"

I recognized the voice calling out. It was Trevor. I wiped away the tears. I didn't want him to see me crying. He'd know the tears weren't for Bill. I quickly tried to compose myself so I could turn around as he walked closer to me. I didn't want to yell so I waited to speak when he got closer.

"I've had this discussion with several people. I think it has to do with your family and Dana."

"So, you came to see me then?"

I could see him wink at me through the floodlights on the back of the building. I felt my cheeks burning. I hoped he couldn't see that.

"Well, I – I needed to check on Dana. I haven't been the best friend to her this year. I didn't see her in there."

"She's not doing well. She's been on complete bedrest because of the pregnancy."

"Thank you. I've texted her, but I guess I need to go see her."

"She won't be at the funeral, either. She needs to rest."

I smiled.

"I won't be either. How's your mother handling this?"

"Not too well. I'm afraid. She always loved him. It's good to see you again."

"Maybe next time the circumstances will be better."

He smiled.

"I'll take you up on that, Grace."

I smiled and walked as fast as my heels would carry me to my car and then I just sat there. What did I just say – next time. Why did I say that? I called Dana.

"Do you mind if I stop by?"

"No, please do," she said. Her voice was full of tears.

I got to Dana's and knocked. She told me to come inside. There was no one there except Dana – no Dana's mother; no Lily. There was only Dana sitting in the dark with all the lights out.

"I'm on the couch," she said.

I went over and sat next to her. I put my arm around her.

"Why are you in the dark, Dana?"

I turned on the light. She winced and covered her eyes.

"I just want to be alone. I lost the baby."

"I'm so sorry, Dana. Where's Lily?"

"She's with my mother. I've lost everything."

Dana started to sob. She put her face in her hands.

"I'm sorry."

She looked at me.

"People are right, you know. I'm better off without Bill. I'd just always wanted two children, and now..."

She started crying again.

"It's okay, Dana. You have Lily."

"I know. I don't know what I'd do if she was taken away from me."

I put my arm around her and sat close.

"Thank you, Grace. Does your husband have any leads on my

husband's murder?"

I didn't know what to say.

"I'm sure he does."

"Would he tell you?"

"He left me, Dana. He said he wants a divorce."

"I'm so sorry, Grace."

With one arm around her, I grabbed her other hand and squeezed it.

"It sounds like you and I have more in common by the minute, Grace."

"Why did you stay with him all this time, Dana?"

"He always promised to change, Grace. He would for a few weeks or a month at a time and then he'd go back to the way he was. I don't know how he thought he would be mayor. People would be asking questions and putting things in the news media. I don't understand. And now that he's gone, I've been able to breathe some – not much, but he's not there hiding things from me anymore. I haven't thought about the other women and the cheating and the lies. I don't have to worry about him ridiculing me. You have no idea what I went through every day. Everything I had to hide from people."

"I don't understand, Dana."

"I know. My mother kept telling me to leave him, and I felt paralyzed to do it. He always promised me things would be different, and I believed him. And once Lily came, he told me he'd take her away from me if I left. I think I was coming to a breaking point."

I didn't say anything. I just let her talk.

"Did you ever see that show about the women who finally just lost it and killed someone? It's fascinating to me. So many of them were abused, and they just couldn't take it anymore. They didn't mean to in some cases. In others, they plotted it out, but sometimes, it was an accident. I mean it really was an accident."

I stared at Dana. I wondered if she was delirious. I wasn't sure if she was on medication, but she was acting strangely and slurring her speech. I didn't know what to make of it. And the things she was saying.

"Dana, what are you taking?"

She pointed to the coffee table, where there were several prescription bottles. One of them looked like a sedative. I wondered what its side effects were.

"Why?"

"I think you need some rest. Let me help you get into bed."

I helped Dana to her bedroom and sat on the bed with her for a few minutes. It didn't take her long to fall asleep. I called her mother and told her she needed to come stay with Dana. When she arrived, I headed to the house. I couldn't call it home anymore because it wasn't.

10

The next couple of days were a blur. I think I understood why Drew drank. It was a distraction, a diversion, a way to forget the pain. I had even gone to the gym a few times as my own diversion. The elliptical helped me clear my head, and I found that my exercising friends were right – there is a high associated with exercising. Besides, I could cry on the machine, and people would just assume I was sweating. But that only filled an hour or so of the night; otherwise, I sat and watched the hands of my grandmother's antique clock as they crept around its face. At least during the day, the flowers could take me into their world. The scents, the colors, the textures all spoke to me.

Drew stayed true to his word not to come home. I tried to text him after visiting Dana, but his response was short. He didn't want to talk to me. I even tried calling once, but he didn't answer his phone. I didn't leave a message. In my head, I kept replaying his last words to me. And every time, they ripped through my heart like shards of broken glass. Emmie pleaded with me to stay with her, and Dana texted a few times. She wanted company. I just didn't want to be around either of them. At my desk, I pulled out Trevor's card on more than one occasion and stared at the phone number he'd scrawled on the back. Part of me did want to talk to someone. I even put the numbers in, only to delete them. Trevor sent me a hand-written card to thank me for the arrangement I made for his mother and for visiting the funeral home. It arrived on Thursday, the day after the funeral. I was surprised to get it so quickly.

I'd love to take you up on seeing you under better circumstances. I'd like to catch up on old times was all it said.

One benefit of not having Drew around was that I stopped thinking about the murder investigation. I just thought of the hole where my heart used to be. I did try to look up information on Bill's handler, his image guy, Ray Finch, but I couldn't get past the guy's dazzling white teeth, and since Emmie told me he had an alibi, I didn't worry about it much. No arrests had been made. In a way, I was glad Drew wasn't around. He'd be tense and irritable by now.

How could one week drag out for so long? It had only been one week – seven days -- since Bill's murder, but it seemed like months. So much had happened in such a short period of time.

I was beginning to wonder if Beth was ever going to return from Europe, but I was glad she wasn't coming into the shop. I was glad none of them were there. At least Jazzy didn't pry. The other two definitely would pry, and they'd put their two cents in. I kept Emmie at bay by reassuring her that I was home alone every night. I was full of contradictions, and I didn't know what to do. I found it hard to even utter a prayer. I didn't know what to say there, either.

As I was looking over the orders for the day, the office phone rang.

"Grace's Gifts," I answered in the perkiest voice I could find.

"Good morning, Grace. It's Trevor."

I paused. I was surprised to hear from him.

"Good morning. I got the card."

"I'm glad. Mama has a doctor's appointment later this morning, and I'd really like to have something nice for her to look at over the weekend. Could you make something up?"

"Of course. What time would you like to come by so that I can make sure it's ready for you."

"It will be later in the day. I can text you if you give me your cell number."

Give him my cell number. That didn't sound like a wise idea, but my mouth ran out ahead of my brain. I blurted out the number before my brain realized what I'd just done.

"Why did you do that?" I asked myself out loud after I hung up the phone. Of course, there was no good answer.

There was one wedding on Saturday. Jazzy was going to come in to help me on that one.

Trevor's text came in much later in the day than I expected. I'd been watching my phone most of the day, hoping Drew might send me something. My heart ached. How could he just walk away and totally cut me off?

Appointments took much longer than expected. Mama is exhausted. Could you bring the arrangement to us?

Could I deliver them?

I wished Jazzy was here. I could've called her. She would've taken them for me, but I decided to take them. It was just a flower delivery, and I wouldn't be staying. I glanced at myself in the mirror. I wondered if I'd have bags under my eyes forever, and I was deathly pale. I needed color.

I touched up my makeup. I didn't want to look like a mess. Who was I kidding? There was no one to deceive but myself. I wanted to look good. In reality, I didn't want to look like someone whose life was falling apart all around her. I kept hearing Emmie's voice, though, warning me about being vulnerable. I took a deep breath and loaded the flower into the delivery van. I could do this.

I still remembered their century-old home. It was a beautiful place with landscaped yards and a beautiful garden. Well, there was a beautiful garden when his mother was able to tend to it. Her roses were exquisite, and she may have even planted a few seeds that led me to do what I was doing now.

Trevor opened the door before I had a chance to knock. He was dressed in a pair of jeans and a long-sleeved white dress shirt that was unbuttoned at the collar and the sleeves rolled up to three-quarters.

I should've let Jazzy do this.

"Please, come in."

"I can't stay."

"My mother would like to see you."

Trevor took the flowers from my hands.

"They're beautiful," he said. "She will love them."

The two-story Italianate home had ornate moldings and a carved staircase. The rooms were massive. I can't imagine what it would've been like for his mother to live there alone. It would be creepy for me. But it was still a beautiful place. I'd always loved houses with medallions in the ceilings where the chandeliers hung and the beautiful, rich wood floors, not laminate. She had beautiful oil paintings on the walls and plenty of antique furniture. It hadn't changed in the more than 15 years since I'd seen it last.

"When Dad was sick, we made room in one of the sitting rooms for a hospital bed and made it more comfortable, so he didn't have to take the stairs. Mama is in there now."

I hoped she liked the arrangement. She was always making her own creations from the stems in her gardens. This one wasn't as romantic looking as the last one had been. I'd used some white lilies and mixed in some orange mums and other fall colors. I knew it wasn't the stargazer variety, but he did say "lily."

I followed him into the side parlor. It was on the other side of the kitchen through the dining room. As we passed through the kitchen, the aroma of different spices caught my attention. It smelled so good, and as usual, I hadn't eaten. I hadn't eaten in several days. I had no desire to. I realized how hungry I was. The house was a maze of rooms. My destination was a cozy room with a fireplace, though it was too warm for a fire. Mrs. Blake was in the hospital bed. She looked so frail. Trevor walked over to her and touched her hand.

"Mama, there's someone here to see you."

She opened her eyes and gazed into his face. I could see the love in her eyes.

"You remember Grace? You were asking about her earlier."

She held his hand and turned her head to me. She smiled as I walked forward with the flowers.

"Yes, I remember Grace. Sweet girl."

"She made the arrangement from Monday, and she's brought another today."

He showed it to her, and she gently touched the blooms.

"Put it over there. It's beautiful – all the colors of fall."

She smiled and reached out for my hands. I grabbed both of hers and leaned it to give her a kiss on the cheek.

"He spoils me."

She smiled and turned to him.

"Trevor, do you have it?"

"Yes, I do."

He picked up a snow globe and placed it in my hands. It wasn't Christmas, so I thought it was odd. I remembered this piece well. It was one of her special Christmas decorations. Inside, it was the Sugar Plum Fairy, dressed in a lavender tutu, and it played the Waltz of the Sugar Plum Fairy. Their home at Christmas was a magical place. Mrs. Blake brought in droves of designers to make it distinctive, but there were heirloom pieces that made the holiday personal. When Trevor's parents were newlyweds, they made a trip to New York City to see the Nutcracker ballet. From that Christmas on, Dr. Blake gave his wife something Nutcracker related every Christmas because she loved it so much. This snow globe was from the year Trevor was born.

"I don't understand."

"I want you to have it, my dear. I remembered how much you loved it."

"But I can't take it."

She smiled.

"I always wanted a girl who would love Christmas and the Nutcracker as much as I did. I had all boys and now all grandsons. Going with you to see the Nutcracker those Christmases when you and Trevor dated meant so much to me."

"Thank you. I have beautiful memories of then, too."

I got lost in the beautiful object for a few moments. Drew and I had never gone to see the Nutcracker. Emmie and I did every year, though. Now I really wanted to leave. It was an awkward gift, all things considered, but I couldn't deny a dying woman. I watched as Trevor sat down next to her and held her hand. I tried to slip out of the room without him noticing.

"Please stay," he said.

He leaned in close to whisper something to her. I felt like I was invading an intimate moment between the two. It was precious to see it.

I found a chair in the corner. I listened as he sang Amazing Grace to her. It was a quiet, gentle version just for her. He was so close to her face. She smiled and whispered some of the words along with him. I'd forgotten just how much I loved his voice. I wiped tears away as I watched. She patted his hands and motioned for him to lean in. She kissed him on the cheek.

"I'm going to rest now."

"Yes, ma'am," he said. He stood up and kissed her on the forehead before making sure she was snugly in bed. "If you need anything, call me."

He picked up her cell phone and showed it to her.

"Yes, dear. I just press and hold the number 5. I remember."

I stepped out of the room and waited for him.

"Thank you. The arrangement is lovely, and she loved it."

"I'm glad you like it. I should be going."

"Grace, would you have dinner with me?"

"I can't, and I can't take this beautiful snow globe. It means so much to her."

"Calling you here tonight was partially her idea, and she's been giving away a lot of special items lately. She knows her prognosis doesn't look good. She told me she wanted you to have it. Since she didn't have a daughter of her own, it meant a lot to her to take you to the Nutcracker all those years ago. None of my sisters-in-law seemed as interested in it as you did, and I have a ton of nephews who play soccer. There are no dancers in the bunch."

I nodded.

"I'm overwhelmed. I don't know what to say."

He smiled.

"You were perfect."

"I really need to get going."

"To an empty house," he finished.

How did he know that?

"It's not a good idea for me to stay."

"I'm not asking you to spend the night. I just want to talk to someone. It gets lonely here, and I gave my mother something for the pain just before you walked in. It usually makes her sleepy. She's going to be out for a while. I'm doing my best to make sure she stays comfortable."

We had to pass through the kitchen on the way to the front of the house. There was a massive island in the center and a couple of bar stools next to two place settings. He had planned for me to eat with him. It did smell wonderful. I could smell the oregano and fennel.

"Please have dinner with me. I know you haven't eaten again today."

"No, I haven't, but I –"

He looked at me.

"Had plans?"

"Well, sort of."

He raised an eyebrow.

"Grace, give me a good reason and I'll walk you to the door; otherwise, it's just dinner. I'm used to eating alone, but I'd rather not tonight."

I looked around the room, trying to come up with something.

"That's what I thought."

He nodded and walked toward the stove.

"It's nothing fancy. I didn't want you to think that this was a date or something. It's just homemade spaghetti and meatballs – not out of a jar."

I tried to smile.

"I don't have much time for this, but I enjoy cooking," he said.

"It smells wonderful."

"Come have a taste."

He sliced one of the meatballs and held out the fork. He laughed at my hesitation.

"I promise that it's much better than that cake I made -"

I laughed.

"Okay, the cake I tried to make for your 17th birthday," he said.

I laughed harder. The cake was a disaster. It was a lopsided layer cake that could've rivaled the Leaning Tower of Pisa for its bad angles.

"Finally."

"What?"

"You finally gave me a real smile."

I brushed past that remark.

"That cake just looked like a mess. From what I remember, it tasted pretty good."

He nodded, and he handed the fork toward me again.

"I promise it's just dinner, and I will be the perfect gentleman, Mrs. Ward."

One thing about Trevor was that he always had impeccable manners; his mother was a stickler for that. I smiled.

"Grace, I don't have a lot of human interaction. Mama sleeps a lot, and I'm alone. I read or research cooking shows. When I am talking to adults, it's mainly about her care and –"

He paused and glanced at the floor.

"Plans for after when care isn't needed anymore."

I took the fork and tasted the food. It did taste so good, and he was right I was starving.

He raised an eyebrow.

"Just for dinner, and then I have to go."

"That's all I'm asking."

He smiled. He'd won.

"It's almost finished. Would you like some wine?"

"Thank you, but I don't drink."

He nodded and poured some red wine into a glass.

Everything tasted as wonderful as it had smelled. The meal was relatively quiet. I wasn't good at small talk, but for some reason, the silence with him wasn't awkward anymore.

"So, Grace, tell me about flowers."

"That's a broad subject."

"I'm not going anywhere, and it's better than talking about insurance, med dosage and fevers. And funeral plans, caskets, life insurance, cemetery plots, and burial vaults."

"What do you want to know?"

"What's your favorite flower?"

I smiled. Drew didn't give me flowers. I understood because it would mean he was supporting a competitor, but once, just once, I'd love flowers.

"Delphinium."

He shook his head and looked puzzled.

"Delphinium elatum is a rich, royal blue."

I picked up my phone and searched the internet until I found a photo to show him.

"That is beautiful."

"It's a summer flower. It's great for patriotic arrangements at Memorial Day and July 4th. I love the color. It can be so deep. But I also love roses and lilies. I have petunias and azaleas in my yard. I have several shades of azaleas. I wish they'd bloom year-round."

"Is color what draws you to flowers?"

"Flowers make most people smile. I love seeing their faces. They celebrate births, birthdays, and anniversaries. They celebrate friendship, romance, and when it's all said and done, they celebrate a person's life. There's something special about flowers. And they send a message. I love the folklore associated with them – the meanings behind the colors of the roses or certain types of flowers."

"And you never get flowers, do you?"

I looked down at my plate. That remark stung for some reason. I blinked back the tears.

"Sometimes, I make arrangements for myself out of the leftover flowers. I take them home and pretend Drew sent them, but I totally understand his predicament. I own a flower shop."

"My mother has loved them."

"I do pretty flower designs. For over-the-top, wow types of designs, Emmie is amazing. I just wish she'd rub off on me some."

"You're underestimating yourself, Grace. You should never do that."

"Thank you."

And after dinner, he brought out dessert - a decadent chocolate cake with chocolate frosting and curls of chocolate to decorate it. I could only take a few bites. It was so rich.

"What's on your mind, Grace? You have a ton of questions in there. I know it."

I didn't answer at first. I wasn't sure what he wanted me to say. "Why?"

He smiled and took a sip of the wine.

"That is a loaded one, isn't it?"

"I'm wondering why I'm here now. I think you have something else you want to talk about."

"I just want to set the record straight. I know I can't change the way things are now."

"You don't owe me anything, Trevor. I told you that the other day. Nothing at all. I didn't understand at the time, but I do now. We were just kids."

"I've had a lot of time to think lately, and I need to apologize. When you and I dated, I had my mind set on what I wasn't going to do. I wasn't going to follow in the family tradition. I wasn't going to be a doctor like my father wanted, like his father wanted him to be. I didn't want to be like him and my brothers. I wasn't sure what I wanted to do, but medicine wasn't it."

He paused and shook his head.

"I thought my rebellion had won out. I didn't go to Georgia my freshman year like the rest of the clan. But then the hammer came down. It was obvious I had no say in the matter after that. The youngest child, and I've always said I was my mother's favorite."

He winked at me when he said that.

"She wasn't quite ready for me to leave my freshman year, so my dad allowed it for her, not me. It saved a few dollars for me to get a few core classes out of the way here. At least, I wasn't partying, and my mother got to see me. I did study, and I had a 4.0 that year."

He took a deep breath.

"But that wasn't part of his plan, and I had to play the game because I wasn't man enough to do what I really wanted. If I didn't go to the college he chose and follow his dream, I'd be cut off. No tuition or housing assistance; no car; nothing. And I hadn't put in the leg work to research a bunch of scholarships. My acceptance was last minute, and I'd missed a bunch of scholarship deadlines. I know that sounds shallow now, and I'm embarrassed to even admit it. At 19, I'd never done anything on my own. My parents, especially Mama, had done everything for me. The prospect scared me, and I chickened out."

I glanced at my plate.

"And I hurt you in the process. I've never forgiven myself for hurting you," he said.

I didn't say anything. I just let him talk.

"I got my degree. I did break family tradition by not going to the Medical College here for my medical degree, but I still became that doctor my dad wanted me to be. And now, my dad's gone. And Mama won't be here much longer. This isn't the life I wanted for myself."

He took another small sip of wine and seemed to be gathering his thoughts before he continued.

"More people are surviving cancer these days, but some still die. I hate dealing with death all the time. Don't get me wrong. There are things that I do like. I love the patient interaction. I love helping people. But the insurance companies and the red tape and the politics. I hate all of that. And every time I lose a patient, I look at my own life choices and wonder how things might have been if I'd followed my heart instead of doing what someone else dictated. I want to live my life on my own terms, and I can't do this anymore. I had a patient a couple of months ago – he was my age. His story was like mine. He had a job he hated. He had been pressured by his father to go into law, follow in his footsteps. In the interim, he lost the woman he loved because he had to focus on pleasing his father. He spilled his story out to me. He had liver cancer. He drank to compensate for his pain. Four months. He lived four months after his diagnosis."

He stopped talking and glanced at me.

"That was my wake-up call. Then my mother was diagnosed with cancer. What other sign did I need? She has always been about living in the moment and for making amends while you're living. She's giving away things that are sentimental to her. When someone dies, it's too late, just like it's too late to send someone flowers when they are in the cemetery."

I fidgeted, and he smiled, changing the topic of conversation.

"I've thought of so many possibilities. One thing I do have going for me is I have a portfolio that has performed pretty well over the past couple of years, I have some property, and I don't have much of the tuition debt that a lot of young doctors have. My dad had several streams of income and paid for my tuition. I want to travel the world. I want to explore my artistic side. Maybe I'll become a chef."

He laughed, and I smiled.

"I feel like I've wasted the best parts of my life, and I lost the people who matter the most."

He stared at me again. I didn't know what to say. Part of me had felt that way, too, especially with everything that had happened with Drew over the past year. This definitely wasn't the way I'd planned things.

"You may not like being a doctor, but I know you're a good one. I know you care about people."

He put his hand over mine for a few moments. It surprised me.

"Thank you, Grace."

I pulled my hand away slowly and grabbed my glass.

"Are you happy, Grace?"

I wasn't expecting that question. I could feel the tears welling up in my eyes, and I almost choked on my water. Maybe I could compose myself long enough to form a sentence.

"You look like the Grace I knew, but you aren't her at the same time. You don't have the life I imagined you would. What's your story?"

I felt the tears stinging in my eyes. I thought I'd cried enough lately. Obviously not, as the tears began to course down my cheeks. I shook my head. Truly, all I really wanted was a loving husband and family of my own. My own happily-ever-after story. At times, I wondered what things might've been like if Drew had never come into my life and if Trevor had never broken things off with me. I may have been just a kid, but I daydreamed about wearing a long white dress and walking down an aisle with him at the end.

"I have to go. Thank you for everything."

I started to get up, but Trevor stood in front of me to block me from leaving. I couldn't look at him.

"Please don't stop me, Trevor. Just let me go."

"I told you my story; now I want to hear yours. Please talk to me. You told me that I wasn't a psychiatrist a couple of days ago, but you need to talk to someone."

His voice was gentle, sweet; everything that Drew's voice was not lately. Drew used to be calming and gentle with me; now he was only angry and scolding, at least when we were alone, not that I'd talked to him in a week.

Since he wasn't letting me pass, I turned away. There was a beautiful sunroom behind me in view of the kitchen. I walked in there. It was a comfortable room with overstuffed furniture; the kind with extra pillows and cushions so you had a hard time getting up. I wanted to curl up on the furniture, but I wasn't about to get that comfortable, definitely not here. Instead, I sat down and let the pillows curl around me. Trevor followed me and sat on the other end of the couch I'd picked. The room was cozy. It was lined with windows, but it was already dark outside, so I couldn't see much of the gardens. I sat so that I could look both at Trevor and out the window. I didn't look at him, though. I stared through him to the windows and ultimately outside. I stared at the moon and tried to think of something to say. I didn't want him to know everything.

"I've been told I have a good bedside manner," he said in a gentle tone, prodding me to say something.

"I loved how you sang to your mother earlier."

"Thank you."

"No, thank you for letting me in on that moment. It was so precious. I could tell just how much you two mean to each other, and that's a beautiful thing."

I was rambling, and I knew it.

"Remember how we used to sing together?"

"Yes, I remember the things you and I used to do," he paused and winked at me. "But you're changing the subject."

"Like you said, it's easier to think about what might have been instead of what really is."

"And what is reality for you, Grace?"

I wasn't even sure, and I wasn't sure why I was talking to him. I shouldn't be talking to him; not about this. I shouldn't be here. I needed to leave. But I didn't want to go home to that empty house again.

"Reality for me is that I'll probably never have the dream for my life that I wanted. I've lost several babies. Dana and I were due within a few weeks of each other, and well, as you can see, I have no children. After the last miscarriage, my doctor gave me little hope of conceiving and carrying a baby to term. He's actually discouraged me from trying to get pregnant, which is something I kept from Drew. Fertility treatments are too expensive, and I've had my heart broken too many times to try adoption. I've heard so many horror stories about families getting children and then the mothers changing their minds. Plus, foreign adoption is so expensive."

"And that's all you really wanted."

More tears. I really did not want to do this in front of him, but I was tired. I nodded.

"I don't really know what I want anymore. I think that was Drew's dream, too. He always wanted to be a dad, and I can't make that happen. I feel like he blames me."

"I've talked to Dana," he said. "She told me a lot of things about you."

I pulled a pillow close to me and traced the flower patterns with one of my fingers.

"And what's going on with you and Drew?"

I shook my head, and I started to stand up. I couldn't go there, not with him.

"Grace, keeping all of this inside isn't helping you."

"But neither is me telling you."

I swallowed and looked at him.

"Drew lost his best friend last year about this time, and he won't deal with the grief. It consumes him. He drinks a lot, and he left me. He said that 'we aren't working.'"

That sentence stung every time I thought it or said it.

"He told me he'd talked to a lawyer. He hasn't been home since Sunday when he packed a bag and walked out. He won't answer my calls or texts. I never thought this would happen. We were strong; we were solid. Or at least I thought we were."

I cried for a few minutes. I didn't want to cry anymore.

"What I thought was a curse for not having children has turned out to be more of a blessing. I hate seeing children caught up in the middle of a divorce. It's so hard for everyone involved, and I'm glad that I don't have to deal with that at least."

"Would you take him back?"

That was the question I'd been asking myself the past several days. I had been coming to grips with the fact that Drew was right - we weren't working. And the fact that he had left and was talking to a lawyer made me realize he didn't want to fight for our marriage; he didn't want to try to fix what was broken. I just stared at Trevor.

"I love Drew."

"But?"

I nodded.

"But I don't want to hurt anymore. The past six months have been the hardest. He's a different man from the one I married. Things would have to change drastically. I can't continue living this way. There would be some major stipulations to me taking him back. I'm just not sure he wants to work it out, and I can't take any more broken promises."

I didn't look at Trevor when I said that. I could hear Emmie scolding me for being vulnerable, and I'd said way too much.

I stood up.

"I really need to go now. Thank you for everything, Trevor."

He stood up, too.

"What are you afraid of, Grace?"

I didn't respond right away. The question caught me by surprise. I stared at him while I gathered my thoughts.

"Honestly, a week ago, my biggest fear was losing my husband, and that seems to have happened. And today, my biggest fear is – "

Was I really going to say what I was thinking? I knew what I was thinking. But he didn't need to know it. I stared at the floor and the Oriental rug I was standing on. No, I couldn't say it. It wasn't possible. I couldn't still have any feelings for him. Or did I? I was a muddle of emotions, and Emmie was right I was vulnerable. I needed to leave now. I tried to head for the front door. But he touched my arm.

"What are you afraid of now?" he asked.

I was now afraid of what might come next. I felt the weight of the gold band on the fourth finger of my left hand. I was still married - at least for now. And I had made a promise to him before God. It was a promise I wasn't going to break.

I cleared my throat. My voice was a strained whisper.

"My biggest fear is me, and what I might become."

He raised an eyebrow as though he was trying to figure out that statement. It was fine because I really wasn't sure I understood what I'd just said either.

"I need to go."

I almost said the word "home." I knew I needed to go, but I didn't know where I was going to go.

He reached out for my right hand. He walked a step closer to me and squeezed my hand.

I swallowed.

"Thank you for dinner."

I turned and walked away. He walked me to the door. Before opening it for me, he paused.

"Thank you for coming, Grace, and for talking to me."

I nodded and walked out the door.

11

I held back the flood of the tears until I got into the car, but it didn't take long for the dam to break. I didn't want to head home. I knew Drew wouldn't be there, and I just didn't want to stare at the walls. And I wasn't even sure I wanted to see Drew. I thought about calling Emmie, but I wasn't ready for her interrogation. She'd give me the third degree, especially if I told her I'd just spent the past couple of hours at Trevor's house and how I was feeling now. Well, I really wasn't sure how I was feeling. "Confused" was the word that immediately sprung to mind. Instead, I headed back to my shop. There were some things I could do for tomorrow's wedding, and there was always plenty of paperwork to be done. I could come up with some sort of distraction there.

I went in and carefully locked the door behind me. I headed to my office and turned on some music. I sat down at the desk and put my face in my hands while the tears flowed.

"Late night, tonight?"

I must've jumped out of my chair. I turned to see Drew staring at me.

"Sorry, I didn't mean to startle you," Drew said.

He was leaning against the door frame with his arms folded, and he didn't look the least bit sorry. He looked awful. He hadn't shaved in a couple of days, and while the rugged stubble was attractive on some men, it wasn't attractive on Drew. He wasn't happy either. Gritted jaw and narrowed eyes. Yep. He was angry. Great, this was the last thing I needed. Since he got here only a few minutes after me, he had to have either been waiting or following me. I didn't think he cared, so I didn't know why he was in my office. I wiped the stray tears from my eyes. My face had to have been red and puffy with as hard as I'd cried on the drive down.

"I have some paperwork to do. I've been busy this week. There's a wedding tomorrow."

He just stood there with his arms folded and said nothing. He made me more nervous the longer he stood and stared.

"Is there anything I can help you with, Drew?"

"Is there a law against me seeing my wife?"

What were we going to play questions only?

"No, but you've made it pretty clear this week that you don't want me to be your wife anymore and that I'm the last person you want to see. You don't respond to my texts or calls, and you haven't been home, at least while I was there since Sunday night. And let's not even talk about the past year when you've pushed me away at every turn when I try to get into your heart – a place I once thought was reserved for me."

I got up and walked past him into the work room. At least, I could stay busy or appear to be.

"I might have a break in the Bill Andrews' murder."

"That's nice, Drew."

I wasn't enthusiastic when I said that. I didn't look at him. I don't know if I even cared anymore. I went to the refrigerator and pulled out some flowers. I grabbed my shears and started putting something together. I was just trying to look busy. There was no purpose in what I was doing. I wasn't filling an order.

"I thought you might be interested."

He'd taken up the same pose at a different door frame.

I looked at him.

"It's your investigation, Drew, not mine. You've made that quite clear as well. And unless you're arresting me, I don't care."

I looked down at the flowers. I didn't know what I was doing.

My hands were shaking, and tears were blurring my vision. He didn't say anything. I wasn't sure what he wanted me to do.

"What do you want, Drew? I have things to do."

"I came to tell you about the case."

I put the flowers down and stared at him.

"No, you didn't. You've been telling me this whole time that this was your case. I'll read about it in the paper, or Emmie will tell me. Apparently, she's good friends with your roommate. They talk to each other. You, on the other hand, have an ulterior motive."

He pursed his lips and put his hands on his hips. October typically wasn't cold, and the air-conditioning wasn't on, but there was a definite chill in the air.

"Oh, I think you're very interested in the case."

"Whatever you say."

I picked the flowers back up and tried to look busy.

"It's all about that gun. It was a distinct gun, but you knew that, didn't you? Someone told you. It was expensive. Handmade. A fancy gun."

I nodded. He was acting strangely, and he was making me nervous.

"It's taken some time to track the gun used to kill Bill. This piece was special. To be honest, it is a beautiful gun with a mother of pearl inlay. While it's fancy and even pretty, it's still deadly. It was made in the 1930s. You have no idea how hard it was to trace this gun. It wasn't legally registered. I think it was more of a conversation piece than a firearm. I imagine it had to have its own velvet-lined case or something. But it did come with ammo, all it took was one bullet straight to the heart, killing Bill instantly."

He was intentionally dragging this out. I knew Drew, but this wasn't like him at all. His sentences were choppy.

"Whoever did this knew Bill well. Maybe it was a relative or a close friend. There were some of those at the party."

He walked closer to me. I didn't look up, but I could feel his presence. He was intimidating. I knew he was staring at me.

141

"Like I said, it was really hard to trace this piece. It seems to have been made for a Dr. Michael McMullin in the 1930s. He gave it to his wife, Audrey. According to Audrey's will, she left it to her daughter, Harper McMullin Blake."

He said the name of Trevor's mother slowly and distinctly. I hadn't taken my glance from the flowers, but I knew he was watching my every move. I knew where he was heading with this.

"She lives at the same residence where you were for three hours this evening."

"What were you doing at the Blake house tonight, Grace?"

"I had a flower delivery."

"Do you usually spend three hours delivering flowers? Or is that only when the delivery is to the house of an old love?"

I felt sick. I put down the shears and folded my arms against my chest. I stared right at him, trying to muster up my inner resolve. I couldn't let him intimidate me. I took a deep breath.

"Do I need a lawyer for this conversation to continue?"

"Invoking 'your right to remain silent' makes everyone look guilty, Grace. But I need to finish my story. Bill Andrews is sort of related to the Blake family, but he was an outsider in a lot of ways. From what I understand, he stole some money from the Blakes. He duped the elderly Mrs. Blake, who I hear is dying of cancer. He scammed her out of a hefty sum of money recently, claiming some kind of investment opportunity for her grandchildren. But she would never prosecute Bill because she cared so much for him. Also, there have been some rumors about Trevor Blake. He never cared for Bill - lots of bad blood. He wanted to get back at Bill, so he had an affair with his wife a couple of years ago. Hot, heavy, steamy. She broke it off when she found out she was pregnant with Lily."

I could feel the hair on my arms standing up. Drew was standing so close to me. I felt even more sick when I could smell the faint traces of liquor. I looked at him. He wasn't the man I married. In addition to the stubble, his tie was askew. He had dark circles under his eyes, and he was watching me like a hawk.

"There are some twisted stories in the Blake family. Did you know that Bill was Trevor's half-brother?"

"What on earth are you talking about?"

"It's highly likely that the elder Dr. Blake had an affair with one of his nurses. He arranged for the baby to be adopted and then had him brought into his own family. He obviously made up with Mrs. Blake because Trevor is younger than Bill."

That would explain why Trevor called Bill the brother he never wanted.

"Media attention – Mrs. Blake dying of cancer – a very loving son, not wanting a family secret to get out. I think Trevor finally had enough and took the gun to the party, killing Bill. Tossing the gun was a major mistake. It had been wiped completely clean though – no prints. Hard to trace, but not completely impossible."

Drew had just accused Trevor of murder and a whole slew of other things. I think he may have even implied that Trevor was Lily's father. I took a breath. I had brought the snow globe into the shop with me. I hadn't been sure what to do with it, and now it caught my eye for some reason. I stared at it instead of Drew.

"So, tell me, Mrs. Ward, what were you doing at the Blake house this evening?" he asked in a low, deep voice. The one he used when he was infuriated.

"How do you know where I was? Did you follow me? And how did you know I was there for three hours? And what difference does it even make, Drew? You're the one who has gone to see a lawyer. You're the one who left. You're the one who's made it very clear that you don't want to be married to me, and that you are taking steps to make sure we don't stay married."

I wasn't sure where this strength to confront him was coming from. It had to be sheer anger.

"Just staking out the house of a suspect, and then I saw you. I followed you here so the answer to part of that question is 'yes.'"

I paused. I didn't know what else to say.

"So?" he asked again.

"If you want to accuse me of something, then just do it. Don't be passive-aggressive and dance around it. That's not your style."

I think years of Emmie had finally rubbed off on me. I wasn't going to let Drew scare me, and he was stunned. His mouth had dropped slightly, and he stared right through me.

"Did you sleep with him?"

His words punched me in the heart, where all his other words had gone, but this sentence hit harder than the rest. I had hoped I could make it through this altercation without crying, but that wasn't going to be possible I met his eyes, but I could feel the tears burning in mine. I blinked, trying to hold them back, but it didn't work. I wasn't looking away from him though, and I wasn't backing down.

"If you have to ask me that question, then maybe we really are done, Drew. No, I didn't. Nothing happened. He asked me to bring an arrangement to his mother, who like you said, is dying of cancer. I spent some time with her and him. She used to like me, and maybe she still does. In fact, I'm pretty sure she still does because she gave me a gift. I don't know if it's an expensive gift, but it has a lot of sentimental value."

I walked back into the storefront where I'd placed the snow globe on the counter. I picked it up and showed it to him.

"Do you see this? She gave it to me. Apparently, she's giving away precious things to people in her life. And she gave this to me. Now, I don't know for sure, but that heirloom you are talking about may not even have been in the Blake household before it was used in a murder. If it was a precious item, she could've already given it away. Trevor told me she had been giving lots of things to the people who've been visiting her. Trevor's not into guns. So maybe you have your facts wrong."

I put the snow globe down, and I took a deep breath because I wasn't finished.

"And speaking of Trevor, he wants his mother to have lots of flowers to enjoy before she dies. And then he fed me – spaghetti and meatballs - because he knew that I don't take time to eat on some days and have hardly eaten all week. Mainly because I feel like I'm dying inside. I've had no desire to eat. Okay? Are you happy now? And you know I can't lie. You can see it in my face. So now that you are looking dead at me, I'll look you in the eyes and say it again. I did not have sex with Trevor Blake last night. In fact, there wasn't any physical contact except for him to touch my hand as I was leaving. I just didn't want to go home to an empty house again, and he was at least nice to me. He wanted to talk, and he acted like he genuinely cared about what I had to say."

Drew didn't answer right away. He seemed to be summing me up, scanning me. He walked closer to me. I don't think he could've gotten any closer without touching me if he'd tried. Part of me wanted him just to hold me and not be angry at me; the other part was just hoping this sense of bravado will hold up a little while longer.

"You may not have slept with him, but something definitely happened between the two of you."

He seemed to be making a verdict when he said that. I glanced away. Tell-tale sign. I knew. But he wasn't backing down either. I looked back at him.

"Now, you have nothing to say for yourself, Grace? You sure were doing a lot of talking a minute ago."

"A lot of good it's doing."

He walked back to his doorpost and seemed to get lost in thought.

"How much have you seen Trevor this week?"

"Am I being interrogated?"

"In a way, yes, because he is on my suspect list."

"He's been in the shop a couple of times. He bought flowers for his mother twice and flowers for the funeral. I saw him at the funeral home. He brought me lunch on Monday, and he had lunch here, too, at my desk."

There was no way Trevor was a murderer. And having an affair with Dana? I don't believe Dana would cheat on anyone. She was so emotionally broken over Bill. She seemed utterly in love with him. I couldn't believe what Drew was saying, but he must've been doing it to get my reaction. I think he got more than he planned for.

"Has he asked you about the investigation?"

"Yes."

"What did you tell him?"

"Drew, what information do I have?"

"Oh, you know more than you think."

"I told him you were following leads. I didn't give specifics."

"Did you see him at the party last week?"

"No, I don't remember seeing him."

I stared at him.

"You think he killed Bill?"

He raised an eyebrow and nodded slowly.

"I told you you'd be interested."

"So, when are you going to arrest him?"

"I have to be 100 percent sure. I'm waiting for one more piece of evidence on the gun. Did Trevor Blake tell you that he and Bill had words at the party?"

"No."

"They were seen having a heated discussion at one point."

I shook my head. He was deliberately trying to cause me to doubt Trevor and be suspicious of him. Drew was jealous. He was giving me far too much information. This whole time he'd been saying, "My investigation, Grace. My investigation." He had no other reason to tell me this except to get me riled up. I didn't finish my sentence. I wasn't going to ask him what he thought happened. I didn't trust him.

"I think Trevor was concerned about some of the family secrets getting out. Political candidates definitely undergo more scrutiny. Trevor confronted Bill at the end of the party before he had the chance to make the announcement."

I didn't know what he wanted me to say.

"There were a lot of people at the party and a lot of people had motives. I even had a motive and a gun."

He laughed at my remark.

"Reaching to protect your first lover?"

He practically snarled when he said that. If I hadn't been so afraid of Drew at that moment I might've laughed, but his jealous behavior was scaring me. That and the fact that he'd been drinking. I'd never known him to drink during the day. Things were getting worse. Though he'd never hit me, I wasn't sure what this combination of jealousy, anger, and alcohol could lead to.

"Just giving you other possibilities," I whispered.

"Somehow, I think you'll hear about the arrest before the news of the arrest hits the television. And about Sunny. She apparently has a solid alibi for the night of the murder. She's doing the same thing she did the first time she was in business. And Jimmy and Peggy and Ray and Dana and even you. I've done my digging on all of you."

Drew paused. He walked into my work room and pounded his fist on my worktable. The unexpected action scared me. I jumped and then I moved away from him. I didn't know what he might do. He ran his fingers through his hair and paced for a few moments. Finally, he dropped his arms and walked back toward me. I backed up until I hit a wall.

"Grace, look, can we call a truce or something? I would offer to take you to get something to eat, but since you've already eaten, maybe I could get you some tea while I have some coffee?"

I just looked at him. I was shaking on the inside and possibly on the outside. I didn't trust his motives. He was suddenly being nice after being angry with me. Was this what Dana dealt with all the time? He walked closer, but I backed up. His expression was something I didn't expect. He looked so sad.

"I talked to Zack the other day," he said.

"That's good. He used to be your friend."

He laughed.

"Yeah, he introduced me to the best thing that's ever happened to me."

The knife he'd stuck in my heart was still there. With that comment, he turned it slightly.

If I was the best thing that had ever happened to him, why had he moved out, and why was he acting this way? Why was he confusing me?

"I'm sorry, Grace."

That wasn't good enough.

"True repentance isn't just saying 'I'm sorry.' It's changing your behavior, Drew. I forgive you, but I don't trust you to change. You said you were sorry in April. You promised to change. Nothing changed."

As soon as it came out of my mouth, I realized just how harsh it must've sounded, but he'd been harsh with me. His face was a mix of surprise and pain. But I couldn't keep going around the same mountain with him. Something had to give. Something had to change for more than a couple of weeks or a month.

"You've said you were sorry before and nothing changed. Now you just want to keep an eye on me. You're jealous of Trevor. It's okay when you walk away, but you seem to think that I'm having an affair and that makes you jealous. You expect me to just say everything's okay and you can come back. It's okay for you to hurt me and me to let you back in. That's not happening. You have some problems that I can't solve for you."

He was the one looking at the floor this time.

"You're right. What do I have to do?"

"I don't know anymore, Drew. But like I told you back before, I'm not going to watch you self-destruct. If you want to drink yourself into oblivion because you can't or won't deal with the past, then fine, but I'm not going to watch the downward spiral. You are the one who left, not me, and without you there, I don't have to see it happen. What happened to us, Drew? This is not how I thought we'd end up. You and I promised each other we would never be one of those couples -"

I shook my head. I was glad Trevor had asked me if I'd take

Drew back. It made things clearer for me now. Drew had to make real changes not just say he was going to make them. I had to see the changes; I had to know he meant what he said. I couldn't watch his addiction destroy him. It hurt too much, so did being shut out and pushed away. He put his hands on his hips and looked away. I knew he was searching for something to say, but I wasn't quite ready for what he came up with.

"Do you want me to tell you about the day that Mark and Linda died?"

Now I was really surprised. I'd been waiting to hear those words for almost a year. I felt frozen in place. He stared at me, but the look was different this time. He wasn't accusatory; he was broken.

"Come home with me, and I'll tell you everything you think you want to know. Let me drive and gather my thoughts."

His voice broke when he said that. Home. Did he still consider it home? I wasn't sure how to react. Was he going to switch back into the angry man I'd just seen? I hesitated.

"Please."

"I just need to lock up."

He gave a faint smile.

On the drive home, I tried to figure out Drew's behavior. I thought I was in an emotional mess before he showed up, now it was compounded. He was so jealous of Trevor. Why did he want to tell me about Mark and Linda? Was this a breakthrough to asking for help for his PTSD? He could tell me and not necessarily get help for his drinking. I wondered if Mark and Linda were a symptom of something else. What else wasn't working between us? We needed to fix it all or at least put all of it on the table. I couldn't help but thinking about what he'd implied about Trevor. Had Trevor used me? Was he having an affair with Dana? He lived in Charlotte. I supposed it was possible, but it seemed unlikely, especially knowing Dana. Of course, at this point, I didn't know if I knew anyone. I wasn't even sure I knew myself.

I tried to dismiss the doubt Drew was trying to put into my

mind. It started to gnaw at me that Trevor had just shown up at my doorstep on Monday out of the blue after years of no contact, and that he had asked me so many questions. I wasn't sure why I was thinking about Trevor when Drew was going to talk to me. Maybe I didn't really believe Drew was going to tell me anything. I expected him to just skim the surface and not really deal with it. After all, he'd been doing that for the past year. He didn't seem to think it was important to get it out and deal with the grief. I wasn't even sure if it was just grief gnawing at him. Was there more?

He'd stayed to make sure I was safe when locking up the shop, but he still managed to get home first. I found him slumped over on the couch.

"Do you mind if I change?" I asked.

He glanced up at me. He took a deep breath and shrugged his shoulders. He seemed annoyed with me, though.

"Go ahead."

I wanted to get out of the dress pants and into something more comfortable. I had a feeling this might be a long night. I put on a pair of sweatpants and a t-shirt and sat in the chair across from him. I felt empty, like a sponge that had been wrung dry and then left forgotten on a shelf in the sun.

"I'm all ears."

"You and I were talking about vows the other night."

"And I haven't broken them. I already told you that."

"I'm not talking about you, Grace. I made a vow to God on our wedding day to protect you, to keep you from harm. It's a vow I've broken several times now, all in one year. At one time, I could keep my job separate from our personal life. I had a work box and a Grace box. There was a church box and all the boxes were neatly stacked so they didn't overlap. I even tried to keep it so their edges didn't touch. Everything stayed in its own box."

"You told me that a couple of days ago."

His gaze darted around the room. This was uncomfortable for him, and it needed to be. I wasn't going to make it easy for him either. He certainly hadn't made my life easy lately.

"Mark was my friend. Yes, you and I had dinner with him and Linda every now and then, but you and Linda never formed a bond. I wanted it that way even though we went out and had fun sometimes. I didn't want work interfering with our personal life, and I thought if Linda was your friend, those lines would come down."

He struggled with words. He stuttered and stumbled.

"You were my sanctuary, my safe place. Home was sacred."

He stared at me; his eyes pleading with me.

"When you started dreaming that Mark was abusing Linda, I moved the Grace box away from their boxes."

He gave me a weak smile.

"I know you don't make these things up, but Mark was my partner; he was my best friend. I knew him - or at least I thought I knew him. There was no way my best friend was abusing his wife. Wouldn't I see the signs?"

He paused and swallowed hard.

"I looked for evidence of abuse. I would sometimes go over there when you had a weekend wedding. I watched college football with them and baseball games, and you knew that. I didn't hide anything. I watched them more than I watched the game. They were good at hiding it for a while."

He glanced at me.

"When his dad died in March, Mark started changing. The changes in the spring were minor. I didn't see them much over the summer. They were at the lake a lot. We all got together for the Fourth like we always did. You and Linda always seemed to get along, but this year, I noticed she was different, and so did you. The dreams started not long after that, if you remember."

He glanced at me again and I nodded. He stood up and started to pace. That wasn't Drew. This whole thing was uncomfortable to him, but I knew he needed to get this out. Holding it in wasn't helping him. I didn't say anything. I waited for him to continue.

"I don't know what happened over the summer, but Mark had gone down fast. I was there for the first Georgia game of the season. Mark usually had a couple of beers during the game. Nothing major. This time, I lost count of how many beers he had. Linda was agitated, and it got worse as the game went on. When it was over, she acted like she didn't want me to leave. She asked if I could stay for dinner, but by then, you were off. I was torn because you were pregnant, and I needed to be with you. I was worried about you because I knew how afraid you were. You should've been at home taking care of yourself, not trying to run a business. I should've stepped in and made you get extra help."

He paused from his steps to look at me. He seemed to want me to say something.

"You don't know how important you are to me, Grace. I was distracted, and I wasn't as observant as usual. Now, it's clear as day, but then, it wasn't. I didn't realize how scared Linda was of him."

A deep breath followed him shaking his head. He walked over to the fireplace, placing both hands on the mantle as he stared at the floor.

"I went back the next few Saturdays. I was worried about him. Your dreams kept coming. You kept seeing there was something wrong, and I was looking for that something. But Mark was smart. He knew Georgia's law. He knew if there was any evidence of abuse, I could arrest him. I had to arrest him. She had no bruises, but I saw her slipping away. Anytime I'd ask if she was okay, she'd say something like 'It's been hard since Mark's daddy died.' And that was it. My gut and your gut told me, and I didn't listen."

He turned to face me again, leaning against the mantle with his arms folded across his chest. He kept shaking his head.

"Some detective I am. I'm a fraud, Grace. I shouldn't be in this line of work. This was right under my nose, and I did nothing."

I didn't know what to say to that. I guess that's the reason he didn't like me in the middle of his cases, not that I really wanted to be in them. He walked over to me and kneeled in front of me.

"I'm not the man you think I am. I should've seen. I should've listened to you more. I should've saved her."

I wanted to console him, but I didn't know how. I also didn't want to stop him. In my heart, I felt that if he could just get these emotions out, it would help him. I wanted to help him; he was my husband. He stood back up and paced with his hands on his hips.

"About a week before the shooting, Linda called me, frantic. She was crying. She was scared. You were working, and I went to their house. He'd hit her. She had a bruise on her face, and I could arrest him. I could put him behind bars."

"You didn't – "

"I didn't tell you because I didn't want you worried. You were already worried enough with the baby. You didn't need anything else on your plate."

I nodded. I was scared the entire pregnancy for as long as it lasted. The dread and fear that I'd lose another baby was always there, and my fear came true. I wasn't sure I could handle that again.

"He was behind bars. Linda asked me to help her get away. We worked on a plan, but we didn't work fast enough. I was trying to help her get some money together. Mark had cut her off from all her friends, and her family wasn't nearby. She didn't want anyone to know what was going on. She wanted to leave Augusta quietly. I found a safe place for her to stay for a couple of days. The plan was for me to take the day off and drive her to the Georgia-Tennessee border, where her sister would pick her up."

He stopped and turned. I could see the tears rolling down his cheeks.

"Mark thought Linda and I were having an affair because of the way she paid attention to me when I was there watching football. He'd become obsessive and paranoid. When he got out of jail, he called her, begging for forgiveness, promising it would never happen again. She didn't go home right away, but she did go home."

He sat down and covered his face. I wasn't sure how to feel about all of this. So many things he'd kept from me under the guise of trying to protect me. I felt sick. I had no idea he was going through all of this. I was so consumed with what had been going on with me that I missed it.

"That night, he beat her. She called me the next morning. She thought he was asleep. We were supposed to leave that day."

He paused and stared off into space for a few moments. I could tell what he was thinking. I knew he was thinking "if only."

"He heard her on the phone. Her cry for help to me. In his mind, that was confirmation of what he thought - that I was having an affair with her. I could hear her crying in the background, telling him it wasn't true. I heard him slap her."

He took another deep breath. I think he was trying to control the tears. I'd never seen my husband like this. I thought all of my tears had been cried, but as I watched the anguish, I realized I was wrong. My heart ached for him, and there was nothing I could do. Tears poured down my cheeks as I listened to his story.

"I put him on speaker and texted Butch to get people out to their house and that I was on the way. I had to keep him on the phone. If I could keep him on the phone, I could keep her alive. At least, that's what I thought. I told him about you and the baby. I told him there was no way I'd do anything to hurt you or him or Linda. He was my friend, Grace," he said as he looked straight at me. His eyes begged me to stop the pain. Yet, I felt frozen in the chair. This was the same man who kept pushing me away, the same man who had accused me, the same one.

"He was angry. He blamed me for putting him in jail and ending his marriage and career," he continued. Drew's voice rose as his own anger poured out of him.

"I got to the house. He'd barricaded them inside. He didn't plan to come out alive. I begged him to let her go. It didn't have to be this way. He didn't have to hurt her. Other deputies arrived. It was a hostage situation."

Another pause; another glassy stare.

"Finally, after what seemed like forever on the phone, I

convinced him to let her out," his voice was flat. "The door opened, and he pushed her out. She fell down the steps of the porch. She picked herself up and started to run, and he – "

Drew swallowed and exhaled slowly.

"He shot her and turned the gun on himself. There were other bullets ringing out. I don't know who was shooting. All I saw was the look of fear and horror as she was hit and fell to the ground. Mark was an excellent shot. He was a sniper in the military before he became a deputy. He didn't miss. She died instantly."

His eyes darted back to me. I felt numb as I stared at him.

"It's my fault they're dead, Grace. Mine, all mine. I should've –"

"What? You arrested him. You put him behind bars. You were his friend. You tried to talk him out of it. You tried to get her out of town. You didn't pull the trigger."

"It wasn't enough, and now, I've become him. I drink to drown out her face. I drink to drown out what a failure I am. I have a wife who all she ever wanted was to be a mother, and we have no children. I'm a fraud at my job. I didn't tell them the whole truth, Grace. My report said nothing about Mark accusing me of having an affair with Linda."

"Did you?"

He acted as though I'd slapped him.

"No, I'd never cheat on you, Grace. How could you - "

I raised an eyebrow.

"And I'd never cheat on you either, Drew," I whispered.

He nodded.

"I know. I'm sorry. I should never have accused you of that."

He stood up.

"I'm tired, and I need to go."

"It's late. You can stay here. This is still your house, you know."

He narrowed his eyes at me. I wasn't sure why I'd said it either. It just came out. But I knew I wasn't going to do what I'd done the last time to keep him with me.

"No, it's best for me to go. I can't deal with this. I know the way I deal with it isn't helping me, but it's the only way to erase the pain. At least it goes away for a while."

He started to head toward the door, but he paused at my chair. I stood up. I wasn't sure what to feel, but I did share the overwhelming emptiness he was feeling. He reached out and gently touched my face.

"I never wanted this life for us," he said. "I promised you so much more, so much better."

With that, he walked out the front door.

I grabbed my phone.

Drew told me about what happened with Mark and Linda.

I texted Zack. Despite the late hour, he responded.

And?

He's a mess. He left. I think he has a date with a bottle tonight.

Thanks for the warning, sis. I'll reach out to him. Are you okay?

I don't know what okay is.

Take care of yourself. I'll talk to you later.

I crawled under the covers and cried myself to sleep. I didn't sleep much. I tossed and turned and dreamed all night of a drowning Drew and not being able to save him.

The next morning, I threw on some clothes without looking at myself in the mirror. I had makeup at the shop. I could put some on there so I didn't look like a zombie or vampire. Halloween was only a few days away – what did it matter? It wasn't on the way to the shop, and even though I figured Drew was following me, I drove past Trevor's house. Dana's car was out front. I felt Drew's words reverberating, and I tried not to let them bother me. They were related - sort of. I tried to shake it off. What difference should it make to me if Dana was there? He and I didn't have a relationship. I was married. I needed to focus. But could Trevor have helped her? Or was Drew just telling me that to get a reaction out of me? Would he give me a play by play before he made an arrest? He wasn't always too big on sharing details unless I had some knowledge of them. I wish I knew what was really going on, but for now, I was going to focus on a college football themed wedding. Yes, you've got it folks. I live in the South; it's the middle of college football season, and this lovely couple's favorite team has the weekend off so they decided to squeeze their nuptials in on bye day. It's an orange and purple kind of day when two Clemson Tiger diehards tie the knot.

This wedding was an afternoon affair. It would be an intimate one and would be beautiful despite the fact that orange with purple were the bride's choice of colors. They weren't my favorite color combination, but it wasn't my wedding. I was glad I wasn't doing the cakes. They followed the theme, of course. The groom's cake was supposed to look like Death Valley, the nickname for Clemson's stadium. A cake artist, I was not, but I imagined if Emmy or Jazzy put their minds to it they could create some incredible cakes. Maybe I should expand my business to cover cakes and flowers. An added stream of income. I might need that. It was hard enough with both Drew and my salary combined. Of course, he'd been siphoning money off for months for alcohol and maybe with plans of starting a new life, so that wouldn't be a problem any longer.

Jazzy had come in to help me with the final details.

"Orange and purple. I never really thought those colors went together, but when you link them with some red, it's much better."

I smiled.

"You can get in trouble with shades of red around here. Carolina is garnet, Alabama is crimson, and Georgia is red."

Jazzy laughed.

"Well, those two colors – they just aren't right."

"Don't tell the bride that, okay? It's all right to put some white in there, but stay away from the red."

"Is that the reason Emmie didn't help you with this one?"

"Yes, she boycotts college themed weddings unless Georgia is one of the teams. And we've actually done a few."

"Don't you have a big Bulldog wedding coming up?"

"Yes, I talked to a bride about a Georgia wedding, but it's not until January, after the Sugar Bowl."

"My grandmother used to have a sugar bowl. It had sugar it in for her coffee. I don't know anything about any bowls except for the ones you eat cereal out of," Jazzy said, trying hard not to laugh.

"Well, don't tell anyone about that around here. If anyone says Georgia is going to the Sugar Bowl or the Rose Bowl or some bowl, you should smile at them. They will be very happy people. Just don't add any red to those flowers. They will not be happy. Trust me."

"Speaking of red. Miss Grace, you could use some color this morning. You know I'm good at flowers, but I'm also pretty good with makeup."

I smiled.

"You know you don't have to call me 'Miss Grace.' You can call me 'Grace.'"

"My grandmother told me it was a sign of respect for my elders."

"Thanks, Jazzy. Thanks a lot."

"Not saying you are old, but are you okay today?"

"No, Jazzy, but I'm sure I will be okay."

"Let me give you a little color."

I know it was a really awful thought that crossed my mind, but Jazzy was a prostitute not that long ago. The last thing I needed was to look like a prostitute.

"I promise not too much," she smiled at me and put her hands on her hips. "Shug, I know what you were thinking. Your face said it all."

"I'm sorry, Jazzy."

"No need for that. I've left that life behind, and you know it. I promise not to make you look like a prostitute."

I laughed. I agreed and entrusted my face in her hands. And she was true to her word. Better yet, I didn't look like a vampire or a zombie anymore. She hid my bags and dark circles. I could be presentable around customers today. It was a little more than I would put on myself, but there was something about it that made me feel good, confident. I stared at my reflection. I didn't look like the same woman, but then again, after the week I'd had, I wasn't the same woman.

"Jazzy, that's amazing. I look and feel like a movie star. You need to teach me how to do that."

She smiled.

"Honey, it's all about shading and brush techniques. You don't have to pile it on; you just emphasize what you've got, and you've got great bone structure."

I gave her a hug.

"You need to open your own shop. Jazzy's Flowers and Makeup Salon or something."

"One thing at a time. First Augusta Tech, then the world."

"That sounds like a good plan."

We still had a little bit of time before we had to leave for the wedding. There was something I was forgetting for this wedding. My to-do list for this morning was missing so I picked up my phone to see if I'd taken a photograph of it or anything that would remind me of all that needed to be done. I picked up my phone. I hoped for a text or something from Drew, but there was nothing. I wasn't sure why I was bothering at this point. I scrolled through my photos and came across one I didn't expect. I had a horrible habit of taking pictures of the floor or something random because I hadn't closed my camera out. On the night of Bill's murder, I decided to take a couple of photos in the party before I heard Dana screaming, I didn't realize it, but I had taken several photos of the scene including one of her over Bill's body. Something was odd about the photo though. There was something different about her. It sent a chill down my spine, and the hair on my arms stood up. I stared at the photo for several minutes. It was a gruesome scene, but I couldn't take my eyes off it. Who had killed him? Did Trevor kill him? In my heart, I knew it couldn't be true, but what if he had?

I didn't have time to figure it out before I heard the front bell ring. I looked up to see Trevor walking in the door. My first thought went to a documentary I'd watched a few weeks ago. It was about serial killers and how several of them were good-looking, charming, and intelligent. All that described Trevor, but we were talking about one murder here of a total jerk, not seduction and then grisly murders of multiple women.

"Grace. You look incredible," he said as he walked to my counter.

I wasn't sure what expression I had on my face as I stared at him. I wondered where my gun was. In April, I'd been tricked into believing I was helping a young girl get out of prostitution when she was actually running the whole operation. I wasn't the greatest judge of people, apparently. I hesitated in responding.

"Thank you."

I could hear Drew's voice echoing in my brain – all the things he'd said about Trevor, the murder, the affair, the fact that Bill was Trevor's half-brother. I didn't believe him, or did I? I felt nervous and anxious and for different reasons than I had before. More than anything, I had a harder time believing Dana had an affair with anyone.

"I have to leave for a wedding shortly."

That was partially true, but I didn't want to be here with him.

"Is something wrong?"

I shook my head.

"No, everything is fine. If you'll excuse me, I have to get ready for the wedding."

I walked past him into the back of the shop to load the van. He followed me.

"Let me help you."

I shook my head again.

"No, really, it's fine. I have Jazzy here with me."

I pointed to Jazzy, who scowled at me but waved at him.

"Miss Grace, I can take these for you."

I turned to face her and glared at her, but she ignored me. She picked up the altar arrangement and headed to the van.

"Did I do something?" Trevor asked.

"No, you're fine. I just have to work. Why are you here?"

I glanced around as Jazzy came back in to get more of the flowers.

"I wanted to check on you after last night."

I looked at the floor.

"Old Government House, right?" Jazzy came back in again.

"Yes, is everything loaded already?"

"Yes, it's all ready to go. I got this. I talked to the bride's mother yesterday, remember?"

I nodded and followed her out the door. And I was alone with a possible serial killer, or at least a possible murderer. She waved at me as she drove away. Trevor was behind me. I swung back around. Why was he here?

"How's your mother doing this morning?"

"She's comfortable. Dana usually stops by with the baby, and this is the first time she's been in a couple of weeks. Her mother brought her today after I got a visit from your husband."

I stared at him. Drew hadn't arrested him. Did that mean anything?

"Oh."

"And it appears that you talked with him recently, too."

"Why do you say that?"

"You're scared of me, and I don't know why."

I didn't answer. I just stood there frozen.

"After the way he raked me over the coals this morning, I was worried about you, and I think I was right to be concerned," he said.

"Why? I'm fine."

"No, you're not fine, and I'm really sorry about last night."

"What about last night? Nothing happened last night."

He raised an eyebrow.

161

"No, you're wrong. A couple of things did happen, and your husband thinks a lot more happened."

I didn't know what to say, so I blurted out the first thing I thought of.

"He accused me of sleeping with you, and he didn't believe me when I said I didn't. He told me several times that I'd spent three hours inside your house. I guess he thinks sex is all that can happen during that time. Of course, it doesn't help that – "

I stopped myself from rambling. I think both of us were well aware that not all our feelings for each other had completely gone away, but I didn't need to point it out, not now anyway.

"It doesn't help that we once had a relationship, and he's pointed that out several times as well," I rephrased my statement.

He nodded.

"Are you okay, Grace?"

All I could read from Trevor was his concern for me. I started to drop my guard a little.

"No, I'm confused and scared."

I took a deep breath. I still wanted him to leave.

"Is that the only reason you came here this morning, Trevor? I have a lot to do and -"

"No. It's not the only reason I came. Are we going back inside, or are we going to have this conversation in your parking lot?"

I shook my head.

"It's obvious my husband is watching us. For all I know, he's listening, too, which is the reason we are standing out here. For that matter, my phone could be bugged. I don't know."

"Sounds like you had a rough night."

"You could say that."

I wasn't sure who to trust right now or what to say.

"What did Drew come to see you about?"

"Let's go inside, Grace. I don't think he's bugged your office or else he'd know the conversations you and I have had."

I headed into my office. At least there were chairs there. Once inside, Trevor told me about Drew's visit.

"He was asking about a gun – a very specific gun that belonged to my mother."

I nodded.

"He wanted us to ID it, so we did."

"He told me it was the murder weapon. How did a murderer get your mother's gun if it was locked up in your house?"

"Ah, you think I killed Bill? That's the reason you're acting this way."

"I don't know what or who to believe, Trevor. Drew's convinced you killed Bill."

"I want you to look directly at me and ask me that question."

He was sitting in the chair facing my desk, and he leaned over so I could stare into his deep blue eyes. He always had the most beautiful and expressive eyes. He had always been an open book, but that was so long ago. He could've changed; people do.

"Did you kill Bill?"

Either he was a psychopath, or he was telling me the truth when he said "no." No tells, no twitches, no looking away, nothing.

"No, Grace. I did not kill him, and before today, it had been years since I even laid eyes on that gun."

He stressed the word "not."

"Did you have an affair with Dana?"

His expression was like that of a 5 year-old when asked if they liked Brussel sprouts. It was a mix of shock and disgust.

"What? Why would you even think to ask me that?"

Since he had no time to prepare for that question, I went on his visceral response. I shrugged my shoulders.

"Drew told you that too, didn't he?"

I nodded, and Trevor let out a deep sigh.

"I told you I wasn't seeing anyone. I haven't seen anyone in several months now. Women usually want me because of the prestige of being with a doctor or because they think I make a lot of money. I haven't found too many women that wanted me just for me. That's why relationships don't last long. I usually find out what they are after early on."

"I'm sorry. Why do you keep asking me about this investigation? And why did you show up in my shop after all of this time without ever saying a word to me since you broke up with me all those years ago? And why didn't you tell me you had an altercation with Bill on the night of the murder?"

He wrinkled his brow.

"Okay. Slow down. I thought I'd answered these questions last night. First question about the investigation is because of Mama. Look, whoever did this did my family a great favor. There are secrets - family secrets - that would devastate her. Things that my father did; things that Bill has done. And you know that radio guy. What's his name? His first name is a city in Texas – Dallas, Tyler, Austin, Antonio? Whoever he is, he eats politicians for breakfast. Anyway, if Bill ran for mayor, the secrets that would come out would devastate my mother. I wanted her last days to be drama-free."

"Like Bill being your brother?"

He gave me a grim smile.

"Your husband is very good at his job, all the more reason that you believe him and not me."

"So, it's true?"

"My brothers and I suspected it for a while, but Bill found his birth mother a few years ago. She told him the truth. She moved out of the area, had him, and Dad pushed her to give him up for adoption. Bill wanted 'his share' of our family's money as he put it. He vowed silence until after Mama died. It would've devastated her. She was devoted to Dad."

"Does Dana know?"

"I'm sure Bill told her, but it's never come up. Like I said, we agreed to wait until after Mama died."

"It could come out in a trial though."

"Possibly, but trials take a long time. Mercifully, Mama probably won't be here to see all of that."

"Sounds like you had lots of reasons to kill Bill, and you had access to the murder weapon."

"And so did my three brothers and my mother."

"Drew has made me paranoid."

"I can see that. And as for the second question, I'm at a crossroads in my life with Mama's illness. We talked about this last night. She's asked about you. She's asked me how I felt about you, and she even apologized for siding with Dad. She said she was sorry she cost me my happiness. Dana told me things weren't going smoothly between you and Drew. I saw you last week, and I just wanted to talk to you. I wanted to clear the air. You were the last woman I met who wanted to be around me for me, not for what I could give her. And I know you are in no position to have a relationship right now. With you, I know you don't have an ulterior motive. You don't want anything from me, and I know you can't give me anything either. And right now, all I really want is a friend. Nothing more."

I took a breath.

"I'm sorry, Trevor."

"Don't be. I told you I needed to apologize to you and explain, and I've had that opportunity. And I hope we can be friends. I think you could use one right about now as well. And as for the altercation, as you called it, I tried to convince him that his political career was ludicrous and to keep him from making an announcement. In typical Bill fashion, he told me off – rather loudly, I might add."

"What party did I go to? I missed all the altercations with you and Ray Finch and God knows who else."

He chuckled, and I took a deep breath.

"So back to the investigation, how did your mother's gun end up being the weapon that killed Bill?"

"I don't know. Mama said she hadn't seen the gun in years. From what we both remember, it was locked in a velvet-lined case in Dad's study. She sealed off that room when he died. No one ever goes in there. I'd forgotten she had it. We went in there and found the spot where he kept the gun. It was empty. Drew dusted the area for prints."

I nodded.

"Still, it doesn't clear you though, does it?"

"No, it doesn't clear me. It's obvious Drew wants to put me behind bars. I didn't kill Bill, but I can't say that I'm sorry he's gone," his voice trailed off. "I tried to talk him out of it – the whole mayor thing. Dana tried to talk him out of it. My brothers tried to talk him out of it."

"And you weren't having an affair with her?"

"Drew sounds like he's trying to poison you against me, and I totally get it. He's jealous. I can tell, but it sounds like he really doesn't know what he wants when it comes to you."

"You're good. Maybe you could be an investigator."

He smiled.

"No, but I am observant. I'm not a trained psychiatrist, but I've learned a lot about people. And I believe your brother hit the nail on the head with his PTSD diagnosis, even though he's not a doctor."

He paused and narrowed his eyes at me.

"What else did Drew say to you, Grace? That I'm only seeing you to get information from you; that I'm just using you."

"Yes."

"Grace, I'll give you my professional opinion right now. You need to talk to someone and not a layperson. You need to go to a licensed counselor."

I started to say something. Did he think I was crazy?

"Let me finish. I see how you're responding. You have been through a lot in the past year. Remember the key word in PTSD is 'traumatic.' You've been through a lot of trauma in the past year too. You've told me that, seeing the murders, losing another baby, being kidnapped, watching your husband spiral out of control. Plus -"

He hesitated.

"What?"

He took a deep breath.

"I can see signs of abuse – emotional and mental. If he leaves or if he stays, you have to take care of yourself. And I already know you don't take care of yourself. You don't eat properly; I can tell you don't sleep."

I swallowed and nodded.

"Thanks, doc."

He winked.

"I'll bill your insurance company," he said and laughed. I smiled at that.

"See, I got a smile from you. A merry heart?"

"Thank you. I'm confused right now about everything. I'm sorry. I just need to take a breath."

"You said you'd gone to counseling?"

I nodded.

"Why did you really stop?"

"I did for a while until Drew started taking money out of our accounts. I couldn't afford it so I stopped."

"If you had the money, would you go back?"

"Yes. She helped me work through my emotions, but I don't know what's going on with Drew – "

"What if I helped drum up business for you?"

"That's sweet of you, Trevor."

"I want you to take care of yourself, okay?"

I nodded.

There was a brief silence, and then I realized what was bothering me about my photos. I felt my mouth drop, and I quickly covered it with one hand. Trevor furrowed his brow and stared at me.

"What's the matter, Grace?"

"I think I'm going to be sick, and I think I know who killed Bill."

The words were breathy. I closed my eyes and prayed that I was wrong. I pulled out my phone again, scrolling through them to see if I was right.

"What?"

"Would you take a ride with me? I want to check something out, and if I have to call my husband, I don't want to be alone with him. I hate to pull you into this."

He touched my arm.

"I've already been pulled into it."

"I'm hoping I'm wrong. It could be nothing. I just need to check something out."

"Where are we going?"

"I'll tell you when we get there. Trevor, I'm really sorry for accusing you of having an affair with Dana."

"I've met men who play mind games with women, and I've got to hand it to Drew, he did a good job."

The wedding reception we were doing was at the Old Government House. I had permission to be in the space, even though I was early. This was a huge longshot, but I knew that Dana had lots on her mind. Since she was on bedrest, she couldn't take the chance of coming here.

"What are we looking for?" Trevor asked.

"It's just a crazy hunch I have. I think that Dana killed Bill."

He looked as shocked as I felt.

"What? Dana? Are you sure?"

I nodded slowly.

"I know. It's crazy. Do you think Bill could've taken the gun?"

"Mama said after Drew left that Bill had always admired the gun. I don't know if Dad gave it to him or if he took it."

"Right now, it all points back to you."

He nodded.

"It does, but trust me, I didn't shoot him. I barely went near him last week."

I went through the kitchen and found a couple of plastic sandwich bags, and then I headed into the room where Bill was found. There was a linen closet in the room. I was sure the police had searched it, but if I had wanted to hide something quickly and without someone finding it, where would I put something? I put my hand in the plastic bag and surveyed the neat shelves. Everything seemed to be in order; nothing was out of place. I opened a box and pulled out the neatly folded tablecloths. Underneath several, I found what I was looking for, and I pulled out a pair of white opera-length satin gloves. A cursory search for a weapon and the gloves would've been overlooked, I guess. The gloves had powder stains on them and blood spatter.

I sank to the floor. Trevor looked as stunned as I felt. He slid to the floor with me.

"I can't believe it," he said.

I took a few deep breaths. I just sat there. One of two people was going to jail. It was either going to be Dana or Trevor. Trevor was innocent, but Dana – Dana was supposed to have been my friend. I thought I knew her. And I was going to be the one who turned her in for murder? I bit my lip. I tried to imagine what happened that night. I couldn't stop shaking my head. This couldn't be happening. Dana? Dana of all people.

Trevor sat next to me and briefly put his arm around me to comfort me.

"There has to be more to the story, Grace. You and I both know that. She's not a cold-blooded killer," he whispered.

"I know, but I did overhear her tell Drew she'd kill him if she found out he was having an affair. And on the night I saw you at the funeral home, I went to Dana's. I thought she was delirious, but I think she actually confessed to me. She mentioned something about a TV show where women snap and kill. I think she was trying to tell me. And the day Drew came over to interview her she kept saying 'I didn't murder him.' Not, 'I didn't kill him.' There is a difference. She used the word 'murder' twice."

I tried to figure out what to do next. The right thing to do was call Drew, but I didn't know if I could do that.

"I think I'm going to be sick, Trevor. I'm going to put my friend – my childhood, longtime friend – behind bars. But if I don't do this, Drew will find a way to put you behind bars. He seems determined to punish you because of me. I'm so sorry. You didn't do this. Does he have any evidence besides the gun and the supposed altercation?"

"Only circumstantial. Plus, Bill and I have bad blood. It's fairly well-known. The weekend after I graduated from Georgia, he and I had a fight. I broke his nose."

I laughed.

"I'm sorry. That was inappropriate, but I just can't imagine you breaking someone's nose."

He smiled.

"What was the fight about?"

'He was supposed to be dating Dana, and I found out about him and another girl."

"And she still married him?"

"Yes. He had a silver tongue. He got out of that and, of course, I was the bad guy. It was another one of the reasons I moved to North Carolina and went to med school there. He drove the wedge between my father and me deeper. Over the years, he lied to my mother and manipulated her. And on the night of the party, people saw us. It was only about 20 minutes before he was found dead. Drew knows this. He's got it in for me, doesn't he? And don't be sorry. I'm not sorry to have reconnected with you."

"To say he's jealous is an understatement. I thought that maybe last night there was a glimmer of hope for him and me, but then he shut me out and kicked me in the heart one more time before he walked out the door. I'm not sure how much of a heart I have left."

"We both know Dana had plenty of good reasons to kill Bill. He was mentally and emotionally abusive. He cheated on her with numerous other women. He had all sorts of shady business dealings. With the right lawyer – "

His voice trailed. I knew where he was going with it, though. Maybe a jury would side with her, an abused woman with a young child. She could be the object of their sympathy, and she did have the face of an angel.

"I'll even help her find a really good defense attorney."

He took my phone out of my hand. He scrolled through my contacts until he found the one labeled "hubby." Drew didn't answer the call. I looked down.

"Would you dial his number for me?" he asked as he handed me his phone. I didn't look at him. I tried to fight back the tears. My fingers trembled as I dialed his number and handed the phone back to Trevor. It didn't take long for Drew to answer Trevor's call.

"This is Trevor Blake. I'm at the Old Government House, and we have something you need to see."

I didn't look at Trevor. It hurt that Drew didn't answer my call, but he could take Trevor's only a few seconds later.

I heard Trevor pause.

"Yes, 'We' as in Grace and me," he said.

Trevor put down his phone.

"He's on his way. He said he's right around the corner. Are you okay?"

"I'm getting used to the fact that he doesn't want to have anything to do with me. But it still hurts."

I stared at the gloves. My hands were in the plastic bags so as not to get any fingerprints on the gloves themselves.

"I'm glad you didn't kill Bill, but I hate that it was Dana."

"Grace, somehow I think it's going to be okay. As crazy as that sounds."

"I think it's safe to say that my friendship with her is now officially dead. It seems I'm really good at killing relationships these days."

I took a deep breath.

"What do the gloves have to do with it?" he asked.

"At the start of the party, Dana was wearing these. I was scrolling through my photos earlier, and I found some random photos that I didn't know were there. In them, Dana is standing over the body. And I noticed she had taken the gloves off. I thought it was odd. If she shot Bill, there would've been gunshot residue on her hands, right? But because she was wearing the gloves, the GSR was on the gloves, not her hands. Plus, the gloves covered most of her arm. Also, gloves would mean no fingerprints. She took the gloves off and hid them. And with everything she's gone through medically this week, not wanting to lose another baby and then the aftermath of losing one, she hasn't come down here to get them."

"She stashed the gloves, but I wonder how she got the gun out of here."

"At first, I thought she handed the gun off to someone who could dispose of it for her, but I have other theories," said another voice in the room.

I looked up to see Drew had joined us. Leaning against a doorpost with his arms crossed was a familiar pose. He was glaring at Trevor and me, then I realized how close Trevor and I were sitting together. This didn't look good; no wonder I could see venom in his eyes and hear the icy chill in his voice. I wondered how long he'd been standing there. I knew he'd be upset with me being here with Trevor, but I didn't want to see him alone. And I knew I needed some moral support if I was going to do what felt like betraying my friend. Trevor stood up first. When I stood up, I handed the gloves to Drew. I avoided eye contact with him and then moved back behind Trevor slightly, so he was in between Drew and me.

"I used the plastic, so I wouldn't get fingerprints on them. Maybe this will help your investigation, Drew," I said weakly.

I waited for him to say something snarky about his investigation, but he didn't. He didn't even acknowledge what I'd done, only glared at me. I'd gotten into his investigation. I should've just left them there and done nothing. I guess I did it to get his approval or to prove to me I was important. But what I thought might be some type of victory fell flat, and once again, I ached inside.

"Was the gun small enough to hide on her?" I interjected.

"Possibly. She could've had a holster under her dress," Drew said.

"I can't say that I blame Dana," said Trevor. "She kept a great face, but she wouldn't listen to anyone when we told her to get out of the marriage. This is going to crush my mother. I was hoping it was one of his many haters."

"Drew, are you going to arrest Dana?"

Drew stared at me as though I had two heads.

"I think you know the answer to that. I've got other evidence that ties her to this.

This and your photos should help. Plus, I imagine Dana will probably cave in now and confess. This will be the final straw. I don't think she has the strength to deny it anymore."

"Do you have to arrest Dana? She's been through so much. She doesn't deserve this."

Surprisingly, Drew looked a little sympathetic at my statement, and his tone was gentle.

"Grace, there's enough evidence to support her killing her husband, and I have to follow the law, even if I don't like the circumstances. I can't tell you how this will end, but I know her parents have the money to afford a really good attorney for her. Sometimes, that makes more difference than the letter of the law, and you know it."

"She and her mother are at my house with my mother. I need to get back there and shield Mama from all of this. I just hope she's asleep when you arrive," Trevor said.

"I'll take you back to my shop to get your car, Trevor."

It wasn't a long ride back to the shop.

"Thank you for calling Drew. He didn't want to talk to me."

"You're welcome, Grace. I can see why you didn't want to go alone to the Old Government House. Was he always that way?"

"He used to be so different, Trevor. That man isn't the one I married so maybe he's right. Maybe we're better off -- apart."

I couldn't bring myself to say the word "divorced." I'd been brought up to believe you stuck together through thick and thin, no matter what. I guess that's why Dana stayed with Bill all those years.

We pulled into the parking lot behind my shop.

"Would you mind calling me later to let me know what happens? I know Drew won't tell me, and I know Dana will hate me forever now."

He touched my shoulder. I could see the concern in his eyes.

"Are you going to be okay?"

"Today? No. Maybe one day."

I stayed in my car while Trevor got out. I was glad I wouldn't be there for the final piece of the puzzle to come together. I couldn't imagine seeing Dana's face. I didn't want to hear her confess. I didn't want to see Drew put the handcuffs on her and take her away. I didn't want her to know I was the one who found the gloves and turned them in. But he probably wouldn't do that. It was his case, his investigation, and if he left me out of it, I was more than happy. I called Emmie from my car.

"It was Dana."

"What? Are you sure?"

"Drew's arresting her right now."

"I'll be there in 10 minutes."

It took her five. I'd barely gotten into the shop when Emmie arrived.

"You can't be serious, Grace."

"Deadly."

Emmie had on no makeup, and her hair was in a messy bun. It wasn't at all Emmie-like.

"Sorry, I left a painting to come down here. What on earth is going on?"

I shrugged my shoulders. I wasn't sure.

"It was Dana."

"How do you know?"

I told her about the gloves and the photos.

"Drew said he had a few other pieces of evidence to tie her to it. He said something about expecting her to cave in and give a confession."

The only other questions were how and where did she hide

the gun? And then I poured out last night's happenings with Drew. But this time, there were no tears. I was so numb. I felt dead inside.

"You can move in with the boys and me."

"If push comes to shove, I could put a bed in the storage room. I have a mini fridge and a microwave. What else would I need?"

"That's depressing, hon, and you know it."

"I don't want to upset your lives. I don't really know what I'll do. Let's talk about something else, like when can we have that art exhibition? The holidays are right around the corner. The timing is perfect."

"I've finished several. It's been therapeutic. I have a feeling that I'll be painting more tonight. Do you want to come to my house? You've been alone all week. I've been worried about you. I do know what you're going through, remember? I mean, maybe not the exact same version of it, but close enough."

I nodded in appreciation and gave her a hug.

"I'll let you know. I have my shop. It's my baby. You can get back to your paintings. I'll be fine."

She hugged me.

"Call if you need anything," she said before leaving.

The day seemed to drag on. I called Jazzy to let her know what was going on, and she said she was fine doing the wedding and reception. I knew she would be. I had a few things to keep me busy and keep my mind occupied. I stayed away from my phone, so I wouldn't be tempted by social media to see the breaking news about Bill's killer. I tried to block it from my mind.

Trevor sent me a text that he was taking his mother to the hospital. She'd developed a fever, and they were going to keep her overnight to watch her. He said he'd give me a call when he could to tell me about Dana. I had made an arrangement for the hospital with the intent of taking it over after I closed the shop, but I changed my mind. There was nothing between us, and I didn't want it to look like there was. I could just enjoy them for myself.

I was counting down the minutes until closing time. I wasn't sure why. I even thought about closing early, but I didn't see any point in that. I didn't want to go to the house or to Emmie's. She was in a creative mode and didn't need me to break it. As the clock approached 5 p.m., I turned off the lights in the front of the shop and put the "closed" sign on the door before locking it. I sat in my office and stared blankly at the computer screen.

I heard the bell ring, and I got up to find Drew in the front of the store. He still had a key to the business. I wondered which Drew had walked in. He was holding a large bouquet. Actually, it looked like several bouquets that had come from the grocery store. Not that I minded. I couldn't remember the last time he brought me flowers, although immediately I thought of Jimmy Hughes. The only reason he ever bought flowers was to ask forgiveness. He was also carrying a plain brown bag that smelled a lot like Lo Mein and Chinese chicken wings.

I didn't say anything. I had my guard up. I wasn't sure what he would say to me. I assumed it was a peace offering, but I'd wait to see how things ended.

He placed the bag on the counter without saying anything and unceremoniously handed me the flowers. They were definitely a mix of several bouquets. There were plenty of fall colors, and despite the fact that they were a jumble of stems, they were beautiful. They made me feel warm inside.

"Thank you. I'll go get a vase."

I had to resist the urge to arrange them. I grabbed a vase, filled it with water and plunged the stems in. I could do something with them later.

When I returned, I found Drew at my desk. He'd carefully moved my things away, so we could use it as a dining table. We weren't eating out of white paper Chinese food boxes. Drew had brought plates. Okay, so they were paper plates and plasticware. I wasn't sure what to make of this.

He motioned for me to have a seat.

"You aren't hungry?"

I shook my head, still waiting for the reason behind all this. I was afraid to say anything. I decided to sit and start eating without asking questions.

"I wanted to thank you for finding the gloves."

I almost dropped my fork, but I didn't say anything.

"I had a feeling that would be what caused her to break down, and it was."

I stared at him.

"Why aren't you talking to me, Grace?"

Surprisingly, that statement wasn't harsh, but he was aggravated.

"Because anything I say can and will be used against me. I don't know who you are, and I don't know what will make you mad."

His face fell, and he looked down at his food.

"I have two reasons for being here. I'll get to what you just said, but I thought you'd at least want to know what happened when I saw Dana."

"Not really. Some friend I am. I desert Dana when she almost dies having a baby, and then I find the piece of evidence that causes her to confess to a murder. I sent a friend to jail today, Drew. I don't know if I did a good thing or not."

"You know better than that, Grace."

I twirled the Lo Mein noodles around the plastic fork.

"I really do appreciate your help. I know that every case you helped me on you felt personally involved with. You care. You believe in justice. You believe in helping people. You have great instincts. Don't ever give up on them."

I stared in stunned silence as I searched his face. He tried to smile. I couldn't imagine the look I must've had on my face.

"Don't look so surprised. This is my pathetic attempt at apologizing to you. I know I kept saying it was my case because it was. I don't want anything to happen to you. The first case you helped me with you were almost killed. Don't you understand?"

I nodded. I guess I did.

"And whether I like it or not, Grace, you have been invaluable to me in helping me, but I can't have you in danger all the time. Yes, your dreams are on target. So far, they haven't been wrong. I just wish they'd give us more information sometimes."

I was speechless for another reason now. He'd apologized. He stared at me.

"Do you want me to finish the story?"

"I'm listening. I'm just stunned."

"We've already established that I've been a jerk."

"I never – "

"And you wouldn't ever say that because that's the way you are, Grace."

I glanced down at the food as I gathered my thoughts. I took a deep breath before I posed the next question. I was afraid to look at him, but I forced myself to.

"You mean you believe in my dreams?"

He winked at me.

"Yes, Grace, I do, and no matter what happens, I will always love you."

"Then why – "

He shook his head and restarted his story.

"I got to the Blake house and gave Trevor three minutes. I wasn't sure if he was going to warn Dana or not. He didn't. He was more concerned about his mother. And yes, she was asleep when we got there."

I put down the fork and listened.

"Dana's mother was there, and she was defensive. Dana saw me, and when I held out the evidence bag with the gloves, she broke down. She said she was tired of lying. Her mother told her not to say anything. Dana sat on the floor and cried and confessed. She said Bill had given her the gun to have while she was downtown. She didn't know how he got it. He wanted her to be safe. She had a thigh holster she kept it in during the night. She kept her eye on him all night and didn't leave his side, but not for the reasons you thought. You thought she wanted to make sure he was okay. Instead, she thought he'd be meeting someone at the party."

I shouldn't have turned her in. He deserved it.

"At one point, someone started talking to Dana, and Bill slipped away. She went searching for him. She overheard him talking to someone about his latest girlfriend. I'll spare you those details, but the things he said were pretty graphic about what the two of them did together. She waited until the other person left and confronted him. They went into the stock room, where she said they argued. She said she pulled out the gun and pointed it at him to make him confess. She said she was tired of all the lies. He grabbed the gun, and there was a struggle. The last thing she remembered was hearing the train whistle and a bang, and he was lying on the floor. She was dazed for a minute but ripped off the gloves and put them in the box - where you found them."

He scowled.

"When he wrestled with her and tried to take it from her, she pulled the trigger – whether it was on purpose or not, I don't know. She said it was an accident. Straight through the heart, and since she was cradling him when we found him, she was covered in his blood, which was one way to hide what had happened."

"I guess that explains why you didn't find the gun there."

"She knew we'd have to interrogate her since she discovered the body, or so she wanted us to think. She collapsed at the hospital, and we couldn't exactly interrogate her then. In the meantime, she said she hid in the gun in the hospital room, and then tossed it after she left the hospital. Someone saw her do it and took the gun into the pawn shop."

It was so anti-climactic to hear Drew say everything the way he did.

"Cut and dried."

He nodded.

"She confessed, Grace. We have the murder weapon, gunshot

residue on the gloves, a connection between her and the gun, probable cause, motive, and opportunity. And did I mention she confessed?"

"And Trevor? You just made up all of that to throw me off."

"No. I had reason to suspect him, especially when he started coming around here."

"Are you going to start on that again? I'm tired of fighting with you. I told you nothing happened."

"You two looked awfully cozy in that storeroom."

He narrowed his eyes at me.

"What about Jimmy Hughes? And that life insurance policy?"

"He claims to know nothing about it, but you know that things will be sticky with Dana in jail because of murder or manslaughter or whatever they decide to charge her with. She wouldn't get life insurance money. And we talked with the insurance company. Apparently, Bill took out the policy. They thought it was odd, and he signed a letter saying he was doing it as a good faith gesture to show Jimmy Hughes he intended to repay him for the loan."

"Do you believe that? Or do you think there was something else?"

"Not sure, but I don't think the insurers are lying. They're out of a bunch of money now."

"I can't believe it. I am such a horrible judge of character. Should I be suspicious of Emmie? She's about the only person outside of my family I can trust."

He smiled wryly.

"Emmie's clean. Butch has been watching her for me. But, yeah, you can trust her. And you can probably trust Trevor, too."

I wondered why he said that. He shook his head and changed the subject.

"I doubt Dana gets much jail time, like I already said. Her parents have already ponied up for a high-priced lawyer. And Jimmy has offered to help with attorneys. Dana will be well-represented.

She's been abused. She's a single mom with a young baby to care for. I don't deal with that side of the law, but I really think she's going to be fine, Grace. She'll probably be out on bond in no time."

That didn't help me because I still felt sick over the whole ordeal. I didn't understand any of this.

"And for the next part of my visit."

I think I dreaded this more than hearing the evidence I'd found had sent Dana to jail because I knew what was coming next had to do with us.

"When I left last night, I'd ripped open all those old wounds. I went straight to the liquor store to buy something to ease the pain. I sat in my car for the longest time, though. I stared at the bottle – well, bottles. I remembered all the death and destruction I've seen - the drunk driving accidents I'd been called to, the domestic violence calls I'd gone on. I remembered having to testify at several trials. All of them related to alcohol. So much bloodshed, so many tears."

He paused and stared off into the distance as though he was trying to gather his thoughts. I bit my lip. This had been such an emotionally draining week. I wasn't sure I could handle whatever was coming next. I had already seen him in a puddle of emotions, and when I tried to be supportive and understanding, he lashed out at me. I swallowed and listened. I wasn't sure what else to do.

"I've been staying at Zack's."

That was new information.

"He has that room above the detached garage. I've been there since Tuesday. He doesn't ask questions."

He stared at me when he said that.

"He just sits with me. But I feel guilty drinking in front of him when all he has is root beer. You do know he's been through this same thing, right?"

"Yes in a way. He didn't go into details. He just said the two of you had a lot in common."

"You have a lot more in common with your sister-in-law than you realize."

I didn't answer.

"I went back to Zack's with the full intention of drinking everything I could find. I wanted to drown. I think I may have wanted to die after I relived all the pain last night."

I knew this was hard for him. That's the reason he kept pausing and avoiding eye contact with me.

"I didn't drink all of it. I drank most of it, and it didn't numb anything. It did nothing. It left me wanting more. Zack had convinced me to put in for some days of vacation and I'm going to ask for a leave of absence at the close of this investigation."

"A leave of absence?"

"He was worried about the anniversary. It seems he's talked to you."

I looked away. I was tired of being accused.

"And you're both right. I'm going into rehab. Zack knows a center in North Carolina. It's inpatient, 30 days. They don't just deal with the addiction, but they go to the problems the addiction masks. And they have an area of expertise in PTSD – plus there's a spiritual part, which should make you happy."

"That part of your life used to be important to you."

He brushed that remark aside.

"I can't have contact with the outside world. No cell phones, no computers. I tried doing this on my own, and I failed. I know I need help. Don't worry about paying for it."

He just stared. He seemed to be searching my face for something. I didn't know what type of emotion I was supposed to be having. I'd been on such a rollercoaster ride.

"That's good."

"That's all you have to say?"

"What do you want me to say? I feel empty, Drew. Everything I had to give, I gave. Right now, I don't know if I have anything left. Every time I try to support you, you push me away. You tell me you don't want my pity. I don't pity you. I love you."

"I'm sorry, Grace. I'm sorry for everything I put you through

this year. I'm sorry for treating you the way I have and for taking my anger and grief out on you. I know I can't wipe the slate clean. I'm going up there to check it out and possibly make arrangements to be admitted. I wanted to let you know why you wouldn't be hearing from me for a few days and then for a month. You don't have to worry about me showing up unannounced. You don't have to be on eggshells. You can breathe."

"And then what?"

"I guess that's up to you."

I stared at him. How could he say something like that?

"Up to me? Why would that be up to me?"

I could feel my blood pressure rising and my voice was, too. His mouth dropped slightly. I guess he didn't expect me to be upset, but I was. I stood up and walked out of my office. I tried to take some deep breaths. He followed me. I put my hands on my hips and looked at him.

"Like you've let anything be up to me in the past few weeks. It wasn't up to me when you packed your bags and left. It wasn't up to me when you went to see a lawyer. It wasn't up to me when you decided to take a leave of absence and go to rehab hours away, where I can't even be there for you. You didn't even ask my opinion on any of that. I thought we were partners. We were at one time. You totally left me out of all of it. But what happens next is suddenly up to me? I'm supposed to believe that I'll have any say in a month? Maybe you'll decide to send me divorce papers while you're gone."

He walked toward me and put his hands on my arms.

"You're right, Grace."

I could feel the tears. I just didn't want to cry anymore. I didn't want to hurt anymore.

"I'm sorry. I'm so sorry, Grace. Even though I made decisions without you; a lot of them were because of you - especially going to rehab. When I saw Trevor with you this morning and the look of fear in your eyes, I started thinking about what my life would be like without you, and it's empty. There's nothing. I remembered what

I promised you back in April, and I failed you. I said I would stop drinking. I said I would go to counseling, and you're right - I didn't follow through. But you stayed. You kept your word. You never left me. So, when I said it would be up to you, that's what I meant. I'm not just taking for granted that you'll welcome me back with open arms or that you'll even take me back at all. I don't deserve it. You have every right to say 'no.' But know that I want to be the man you fell in love with."

His arms dropped to his side.

"So much of this has been my fault, and I want to fix me. I can't fix us until I fix me, and I don't know how to fix me."

I touched his arm.

"But I'm part of you. Why can't you see that?"

He reached out and brushed his fingers against my cheek.

"You're the better part of me, Grace, but I've done things I said I've never do and become someone I said I'd never be. And I hurt you in the process. I hate myself for what I've done to you and to me and to us."

His phone began to ring.

"That's probably Zack. He dropped me off, so I could say goodbye. We're going up tonight."

He looked at his phone and nodded before kissing me on the forehead.

"Goodbye, Grace."

I saw Zack pull up outside and watched as Drew walked out the door and got into the car. I wasn't sure what to make of our conversation. "Goodbye" sounded so final, and this felt like the end.

I walked back into my office. I noticed a brown envelope on his chair. I opened it and out slid the divorce papers. He had not signed them, but I saw the spot where I would sign.

"I guess you are leaving this one up to me, after all."

I shook my head. I didn't want this, but I also didn't want my marriage the way it was. I took the papers and fed them to my shredder.

"My name is Grace, and I'll give you a little more grace, Drew. Please get this right," I said it out loud as a hope and prayer for whatever the future held.

www.ingramcontent.com/pod-product-compliance
Lightning Source LLC
Chambersburg PA
CBHW020649260626
47157CB00008B/2971